RT Warner is a first-time author. She is twenty-three years old and currently studying Medicine full time at the University of Birmingham, with only one year left to complete her degree. RT Warner has always enjoyed expressing her artistic side and has strived to maintain her creativity throughout her six years at medical school. Although writing this short novel proved challenging at times for various reasons, she found the overall message to be powerful and hopes that others find it compelling as well.

To Dev

R T Warner

THE MAN ALONE WITH THE LAKE

AUSTIN MACAULEY PUBLISHERS™
LONDON • CAMBRIDGE • NEW YORK • SHARJAH

Copyright © R T Warner 2023

The right of R T Warner to be identified as author of this work has been asserted by the author in accordance with section 77 and 78 of the Copyright, Designs and Patents Act 1988.

All rights reserved. No part of this publication may be reproduced, stored in a retrieval system, or transmitted in any form or by any means, electronic, mechanical, photocopying, recording, or otherwise, without the prior permission of the publishers.

Any person who commits any unauthorised act in relation to this publication may be liable to criminal prosecution and civil claims for damages.

This is a work of fiction. Names, characters, businesses, places, events, locales, and incidents are either the products of the author's imagination or used in a fictitious manner. Any resemblance to actual persons, living or dead, or actual events is purely coincidental.

A CIP catalogue record for this title is available from the British Library.

ISBN 9781398491601 (Paperback)
ISBN 9781398491618 (ePub e-book)

www.austinmacauley.com

First Published 2023
Austin Macauley Publishers Ltd®
1 Canada Square
Canary Wharf
London
E14 5AA

I extend my heartfelt gratitude to Mark for his unwavering support, and I am immensely thankful to the entire team at Austin Macauley Publishers for their dedication and collaboration.

1. The Lost Cabin in the Woods

The thought had first occurred to him around twelve months and fourteen days ago. He had been counting the days away from the thought like he was counting down towards Christmas. It had been fleeting at first, the thought that is, it appeared for a split second, maybe not even that, maybe a half a split second, but what was the technical name for half a split second he often wondered. But anyhow, every day since that initial flicker of a thought, sometimes even twice a day, or possibly, if the day had been particularly bad, even more than that, it would come back. It would reappear in his head without any warning, like a bad memory or a bad dream you cannot stop thinking about, or even something embarrassing you did, you cannot shake it, it constantly reappears when you least expect it, or least want to remember it, it is there, staring you down, glowing red eyes and a Cheshire cat smile, taunting you, teasing you, enticing you.

Kind of like one of those bad memories where you think about everything you did wrong or everything you should have done, all those things you wished you said in a fight but cannot because it has already happened, it is too late and you missed your opportunity, and now the bitter taste of the altercation remains in your mouth, like a stale coffee on your tongue, and the malodour that accompanies it, and you think about it a little too much, you ae too overly conscious of it and maybe you even try and compensate for it, but whatever happens it remains unmoved in your mind for some time at least.

It would creep up on him at any point, when he was at home in his room, or when he was in a huge crowd full of people he knew and did not know, or even, sometimes when he least wanted it, on the pitch, and it would scare him, it would send shivers down his spine and a ricochet of emotions through his body. Mainly because he would not suspect it to come and speak to him, but also partly deep within him, because he knew it was the truth.

Boo! Times up. You're alone here, Thomas.

But back to when it first happened, to when it all first started, that is what most people are interested in finding out about, the reason when and why and how this all came about. How it came to be, how he came to be here today, driving away. Driving alone, in his lavish grey Audi which he did not want or did not chose but was thrust upon him, along with most of his belongings.

It was a common theme, a new shiny watch to match his new brilliant white trainers, to go with his designer clothes and bag that was too small to actually fit anything worthwhile in. Never chosen by himself, never selected by his own hand but hung from his person as if it were a part of his personality.

The same could be said for his car, with its personalised number plate. But it had to be said, he did enjoy driving. The calming peacefulness of being alone, commanding complete control of his ability to go wherever he desired at the drop of a hat, spending hours with only himself and his thoughts, just the hum of the engine in the background.

He enjoyed the feeling of freedom it gave him. And on this particular day, he was driving away, with the window down, the radio off, of course, and the sun seeping in through the open pane and resting on his arms and hands clasped at the wheel tightly, not letting his hand slip from the 10 and 2 position, they were clammy with nerves betwixt with anticipation.

Driving away from everything he knew, everything he had worked towards, all the time and spent emotions he had invested in his life and his future. He was leaving it all behind and moving on, and the best part was, that is, the most tantalising, teasingly wonderful knowledge was knowing that nobody knew he was doing it.

Not one person was aware of his departure, nor would they probably even notice his disappearance. He would slip away into the shadows and cease to exist in the minds of many; he craved the darkness, the seclusion, the loneliness.

It had all begun one morning, when he woke up at around 7:30, as he always did, without an alarm he may want to add, to carry out the day as it tended to happen, he was brushing his teeth, using the harrowing sound of the bristles to deter his own whizzing mind, when he realised that his thoughts were there to help him.

All at once there was a distinct shift in his mind. That this was no longer where he wished to be. He felt an overwhelming and undeniable sense of distance, no, a distaste for his life.

It came from no longer feeling any pride towards his hard-earned accomplishments, or any content of admiration with where he was, or what he was doing with his life. He was not fulfilled with his everyday activities, and the money that he was earning, which, again he may want to add, was considerable.

He did not want to appear ungrateful, as he was sure many young boys and men would, and did, yearn for his life with an ache that consumed them, but to him, he wished for something different. For it is laborious to deny the uncomfortable sensation of feeling out of place.

This was no longer the life for him, perhaps it never truly had been his life. Ever since he had been a child with a talent the vision had been drawn out for him, etched out in the stars, mapped on his life path, all he ever had to do was follow it. It seemed so very simple. Do as he was told and reap the rewards of being a huge success. His perennial trust in those closest to him had skewed his true path. Confusing his dreams and desires with what they wanted from him. A baneful people pleaser. And it had taken him this long to realise that, but no longer.

When he had been permitted to spend his own money, his barbaric nature would take him wild. His usually visualised fruitful purchases with his own earned money used to fill him with pleasure and joy, screaming out his accomplishments with garish bold colours and decorative lines and streaks, but now these too were mild at best and warmed him only for an hour before they too became a bitter distasteful feeling in the pit of his stomach.

He had faked a cheesy, goofy grin for so long his cheeks permanently hurt, it was so used to being plastered there that he barely had to try anymore, he felt like the joker with a smile physically etched onto his face despite the fact he was not happy.

He was not happy at all.

Surrounded by thousands of people, constantly accompanied by another soul, talking in his ear, telling him what to do next, how to speak, how to act. Digitally he was speaking to millions, he was never allowed a moments peace, and yet, despite all of that he was lonely.

He was in the wrong place; he knew this was not the right life for him. But vitally, because he was aware of this, it meant he was aware of himself, which implied that happiness was out there somewhere for him.

It had to be.

And he wanted to do something about it. He wanted to find it. He wanted to feel the same joy and exhilaration that all his fans believed he did.

Although he had tried to push the feeling aside, for months he ignored it because the concept seemed preposterous. This life he had cultivated was the only life he knew, and he was still a child in some respects, he was not sure whether one fleeting instinct was enough to consider throwing it all away, and even if it were he was not convinced the plan he had now carefully detailed and executed was the best way of managing his pain. The burn within him was becoming agony, it rendered him numb, he could barely move without it singeing him, he wanted to escape it with every fibre of his being, but just one held on. Its tendons so very strong, tethering him to his past, for this was the life he had spent years carefully creating and cultivating to get to this very point.

He had so many people relying on him, counting on him, he had the thirty team members, let alone the hundreds and thousands of fans, and yet he felt most pressure from his family. But now, after almost six years of being at the top of everything, the expectations weighing him down and for what?

Something he did not truly care enough about.

He was at the point of breaking. It was all for them, none of it was for him and when that realisation came to him, it was not something he could let go of.

Back then, six years ago that is, he believed he would feel different, he believed he would feel like the man on top of the world, adoring life and everything that came with it. But as it turns out, he was not, he did not feel on top of the world, he did not feel on top of anything for that matter, and he definitely did not adore his life and everything that came with it.

Perhaps this was not the life destined for him.

As already said, it was a great life, do not get him wrong, but it was not the life for him that was clear. As what appears to be perfect for someone is not the same for everyone, but you already knew that.

He thought he knew that.

Now here we are twelve months and fifteen days later. He had woken up earlier than usual, but not by much, he had always been an early riser, but since the incident a few years back he had managed to lose more sleep. He never quite recovered from the pattern, struggling to get to bed despite being exhausted, waking every hour, and finally giving up and lying awake in his bed, staring at the ceiling at around five or five thirty. Watching time slowly pass by, every second a little less painful than the last.

But on this particular day he stepped onto his carpeted bedroom floor at around four fifty-seven, at the first sign of sunlight for the day, creeping across his walls glimmering and shimmering with hope and expectations. This night he had barely slept but for different reasons; the feeling of adventure and excitement that you get the night before a big holiday, or your birthday had prevented him from closing his eyes most of the night.

His heart thumping in his chest, his skin clammy yet covered with goosebumps all at the same time.

Adrenaline.

It kicked in every time the whistle blew at the start of the ninety minutes, and here it was again.

His own beautiful game.

But now he was driving, wide eyed, the exhilaration almost taking over his entire body, sending him into a dizzy frenzy, it was too much for him to take. His body shaking, heart pounding so hard he could feel it, sweat dribbling down his spine, collecting in his underwear where he sat. it felt almost feverish, but he knew it was the excitement.

The elated hysteria he was feeling was because he was now arriving. He pulled off the main road, at least it could be considered a main road compared to the beaten, dirt track he was now driving along, when in fact that road would probably have been considered a remote B-road, wide enough for only one car with tall reeds growing on either side of it, no turning points, only one opening on the left where he pulled over turning the wheel gently through clumps of trees.

The noise of stones scattering, twigs snapping and leaves crunching made up all the sound in the car, rattling and clanging against the metal.

The track was bumpy, he was being thrown about inside the vehicle as its dusty path disappeared; fading away the further he drove. The deeper into the woodland he commenced.

He had turned the radio off around forty minutes ago after hearing his name mentioned no less than four times. It was interesting because he was never sure if he wanted to hear it, he had BBC5Live on the radio, so of course there was always the chance he may be mentioned, but he could have just as easily turned the channel over to Smooth or Magic FM and not heard a peep about him or turned the radio off from the start. There was a small hint of satisfaction in his decision when he heard his name repeated out loud by strangers, he never knew who they were or what right they had to form opinions on him, but they had, and he was desperate to hear what they had to say, it was vain and futile and in all honesty he desired it, and yet did not want it all at the same time.

That was a fault of his, and he knew it, he had craved, desired, and gorged off their opinions, their thoughts, and their wishes for him, despite not knowing who they were. He supposed he would miss the warming contentment of them revelling in his glory or the feeling when he proved one of them wrong or irritated the other by beating their favourite team.

It was all a game in which he loved to win.

The senseless, power-hungry competitiveness had driven him along for the last few years. But it was time to move on from those childish antics, he was ready to move away from that pleasurable cosy feeling. That feeling was the only warmth in his life, and it too was burning out like embers glowing at the end of a dusty fire, holding onto the last glimpse of light. Fading into the foggy mist that was his conscience.

He had arrived, he slowed the car to a stop and yanked the handbrake up without pressing the assist button, the clanking, grating sound echoed around him. It was only then did he realise just how erratic his breathing was. Ragged, shaky breaths dragged from his mouth, accompanying his salty skin, dampened hairline, his soggy underwear.

For a moment, he sat, listening to the sound of birds outside, his chest continuing to rise and fall quickly feeling tight and constrictive as if he had just gone for a run. The scent of burnt rubber filled his nose and made him slightly queasy, he had forgotten to eat something before he left, and now it was turning eleven and his stomach was growling and chomping away at his insides. The churning only adding to his nausea, he clutched at his stomach, squeezing it to try and convince his body he was full. But the nausea rose inside of him, crawling up his stomach into his throat.

Had he made a mistake?

His body's rejection to his arrival must be a sign of some sorts. Something he could not just ignore. The sickly feeling of regret, that he had made a mistake. Surely, the life he left behind would wonder what had come to him, what had come to his greatness and why would he leave behind such a life.

He must be insane!

He often believed he was insane.

He stepped out of the car. The billowing warmth from the exhaust catching the loose ends of his clothes and rubbing up against his skin, caressing against his leg as if enticing him to stay. It was too late for regrets, he had made it all this way and he could not turn back now, not least without trying his luck at his new life.

He had barely himself been able to find this apparent "hidden, remote, lost cabin in the woods", which he guessed was indicative to its name, and so he was highly confident nobody else would be able to. The man, whom he had never met, but had brought the whole small wooden chalet-like building from, had tried to be descriptive in his explanation, but even his detailed instructions seemed vague with the twists and turns of the woodland arena, for how can you describe one tree from the next.

He had informed the man, despite the man's persistence, that he did not want to have him show him the way or around the house, least meet him at all!

The man seemed confused by his request but was hushed to silence with the large sum of money he had forced in his direction and the limited questions asked. He made sure not to mention his real name. Nobody but that man could know he was here, and it was unlikely the man would realise just who he had sold his holiday home to.

Anyway, back to how he managed to find his new home. Well, it was only because of a feeling, following his gut instinct, following a calling of his name and a whisper in the distance, a gust of wind blowing over a hill. They hadn't been calling his name but calling him to come closer, calling him in.

Already he felt more alive, he felt exhilarated. Turning around and around on the spot he tried to take in every colour and light and scent and sound.

It was quiet, the gentle whisper of wind through the leaves and against the floor, the soft mews of birds in the morning and the munching of insects against bark. He had left his car amongst some trees, as there was no parking of course, so it rested in between a series of cedars and oaks which towered above him. He looked up, bending his spine, and craning his neck to glimpse at the sunlight begging its way past the leaves. The nooks allowed the rays to beam through and shone down on his face, his hand lifted above his eyes to protect them and allow him to make out the thousands of shades of green and brown. He took a huge breath in, filling his lungs with the sweet, clean air around him. Of course, it was no cleaner than the little town he had spent the last twenty-two years of his life, but the feeling of a new place made it seem so much cleaner.

But, where to go first? His mind was racing, and yet there was nothing in it, it was empty all at the same time, wondering what to think. He was overwhelmed with emotion and feeling that it was an empty book, a blank canvas, waiting to be filled with everything he could see and smell and taste and touch. He began to walk, away from the cabin he would soon call home, away from his car parked between the trees and away from what he deemed the palace of trees forming his entranceway, he walked away towards an opening.

He had not even stepped inside his new home, but he was moving away from it.

Following the distant calls of the scenery around him. He always felt that the outside was more beckoning, more comforting, less restricted, and he was more interested in his surroundings first.

The light allured him. Its brilliant shine, glowing as it lifted itself into the sky.

He walked slowly, as you always saw people do in films, when they're walking towards something incredible and life changing, or on the other hand, when they're walking towards their death. To be perfectly honest, he was not sure which was reaching out to him.

But he was not afraid of either.

Death had always fascinated him. The way that a single act could vanish someone from this earth, and the way that their life earned work and legacy would slowly fade away into the background.

Most would be remembered for some time, but eventually after time everyone would be forgotten, people would stop talking about you and there will be a last person to mention your name before they too move onto the afterlife.

Death was an exciting concept to him.

He had past associations with it which intrigued him further, the suddenness of passing and the finality of it.

I guess that is why he believed leaving and not telling anyone where he was going or if he would come back was the closest way, he could reach death without actually touching it.

The closest way he could step over the jaws of the afterlife without tripping and falling into it.

That thought thrilled him further, the thought that he was in a completely secluded, unique, and independent landscape, made him feel like his own found heaven; created perfectly for his desires and his tastes. He was in his own, self-made, living afterlife.

The forest land cleared out and made way to a vast water scape. In front of him was a glistening and expansive lake, extending across the valley enclosed within two hills, making way for a glorious and beautiful ravine. It was again ghostlike, not a single indication of civilisation, not a strewn wrapper or coin, not a footprint or a turned log, it was his and his alone, he felt fulfilled, he felt happy and warmed inside. The sunlight he had been beckoned towards was here, dancing out in front of him, Bounding off each ripple of water formed with the sultry wind. This body of water filled him with more contempt than anything he had ever brought himself, or any person had ever given him.

It was strange to think that he felt more comforted, and less alone here, where he was the only person for miles, or so he thought, than back where he used to call home where he was surrounded by people and an expanse of things and a virtual world constantly.

Being there was more isolating and far more chilling than being here.

His hair, replicated thousands of strands of purely spun gold and it was billowing in the wind, scattering delicate brilliant almost fluorescent strands around his head and across his eyes. It hung, typically, shoulder length and shone like the sun, a bright and soft appearing golden blonde hair which he was fond of. Now he was away, he would never cut it, partly as he had no idea how, but also because it would symbolise his freedom, he'd let it grow out and care for it.

He sat momentarily on the bank leading down to the lake, taking every breath as if it was his first, gasping for air and feeling grateful for the crispness and the purity in which it felt.

He rubbed his shins up and down, feeling the cuts and callouses from his last life, rubbing away the feeling and the pain it had caused him.

It was past eleven now, which meant his parents would be awake. How long until they realised, he was gone?

Would they realise at all?

Would they mourn for his absence?

In a second, he was up and wading into the water, still fully dressed, it was bitterly cold, cutting right through his skin to his core. His body feeling stabbed by thousands of razor blades as he advanced further and further in, not hesitating once as the level raised from his ankles to his knees to his torso and chest until he could no longer feel the floor.

He dipped his head under and kicked hard, lifting his body up slightly so he could smooth his hair back out of his face. The water made his body ache and groan, but it was sort of soothing, it felt like he was being born again, waiting for the start of his new life.

He marvelled in the pain. Relishing in it. Some form of torture for his actions. Purging him clean.

This was the sort of pain he would endure now, unlike the physical, mental, and sexual pain of his last life. This life was beautiful, it was pure; he was one with nature and one with life.

Was this what life was about?

Was he about to find out about the meaning of life and the feeling of being alive?

He soon drew weary of the water, and it quickly lost its allure, as he often found it did quickly. His mind moved so fast he found himself outgrowing things rapidly and impatiently, changing courses frequently, tiring easily, concentrating for mere minutes before drifting off to do something else.

He left the water; his clothes clung to his body, and hugged him tightly like a wet sloppy kiss. He did not attempt to dry himself but walked back the way he came, leaving his shoes on the bank of the lake. Nobody was here, nobody would take them. At most he would find a present inside tomorrow in the form of an insect or a dropping of some kind.

That would be exciting!

Entertainment had been his main concern, but he had come prepared. He had brought his entertainment; he had countless books from every genre for every mood and every feeling. He had music, his records, and his player. A speaker and phone were not an option as that required a screen and there were no screens allowed. No way of contacting the last life, no way of hearing what people were saying about him, if anything, no way of reconnecting with the bitterness of social media.

He had his paints, numerous blank canvases as well as sheets and sheets of paper, cardboard, tracing paper, with chalk, charcoal and all kinds and forms of pencils, and pens and paints and oils.

He was covered on that front, with a puzzle in the morning, a Sudoku in the afternoon, and a cookbook to tear apart in the evening he would not get bored. Not counting the surroundings, the vast moorlands with cascading hills and deep, deep lakes between them. His body filled up with elation about the days, months, and years of fulfilment he was going to get here.

His life!

Finally, after spending at least an hour outside in the wilderness, accepting his future being at one with nature, he decided it was time to enter his new home. Somewhere new that was only his.

It was a complete antithesis to his past home, but really what wasn't about this new life he was cultivating?

Unlike the modernised house his parents had built with whitewash plaster, grey slated roofing, bright red brick around the rim of the house. Parquet flooring running throughout the house in one direction, monotone colours and the only ounce of personality were paintings selected for them by an art specialist, so did not even replicate their own personalities, spread across the house on carefully painted, intricately selected, all the same bright, white paint walls.

You would never be able to tell the family who lived there for the sheer lack of photographs; there was not one picture of the members of the family who called it their home.

Not one of his achievements on display, his trophies, his medals, his England caps. Nothing to show that anybody lived there; it was practically a show home. Even his dog was followed around with a hoover to ensure not a single hair was shed on the floor.

God forbid the mess.

His new home was darker, there were fewer windows, and they were smaller in size, showing off less glass than the panels in his last home. Thick borders and windowsills surrounded each of them, and so the natural light was limited, especially as most was shielded from the trees above. It was almost dingy but that made it sort of special, like a cave home almost.

The walls were wooden, like a cabin in the mountains, a ski chalet but reduced in size. Each panel of wood ridged and running in and out of one another. Beams ran across the ceiling, from one side of the room to the other. It was warm and smelled deeply of oak and burnt ashes. The whole building visible from standing in the doorway. The entirety of the cabin could have fit in his bedroom from home, with a small kitchen and sofa squeezed into one corner, across from a bed with a tiny door leading into a tight room with a sink, shower, and a cracked toilet.

Everything you could possibly need was there. What was the point in having useless frivolities, keep everything to the upmost basics and you'll be content.

He kept convincing himself this, he was happy, but used to a lavish lifestyle and so kept repeating that he would not need what he had before, you have everything you could ever need.

You are happy, you are fulfilled.

This is your home now and you can make it however you wish to.

He repeated on and on and on...

He hauled in his baggage, several heavy-duty shopping bags filled to the brim with cans and long-lasting food. His bags of clothes which he had stuffed with every item he did not despite, shoes upon shoes upon shoes. Most of which he decided to leave in the car. Followed by his entertainment.

The trips from the car to the cabin made him break out in a sweat again, collecting around the line of his hair and shining against his forehead and nose.

The last item he picked up from the passenger seat of his car was in fact a football.

It slipped out from his grasp as he shut the boot of his car, rolling away from him and resting against the trunk of a tree. Perfectly timed for a monarch butterfly to land on the skin.

Flashing its wings once before folding up and resting atop the ball.

Though he could not see the eyes of the butterfly it felt as if the insect was looking directly at him.

'What are you doing here?' He demanded of the insect. 'Go away, this is my place.' He shouted. But the butterfly failed to move.

A line of sweat trailed his temple, down his cheek. Drawing him back to reality.

He left the ball where it rest, the butterfly to stubborn to move.

Once he was inside it felt a little overwhelming.

Hs pressed the door firmly shut, sliding against the wooden panels. Allowing his body to collapse against the floor. His knees tucked into his chest, his arms wrapped around his shins, hugging them in. He was surrounded by his belongings.

They felt out of place here, they knew they did not belong within these four walls. Despite his incessant persistence of his belonging.

And for once he was really alone, but in truth he was not as afraid as he should have been, for he did feel he was home.

2. What Does It Feel Like to Be Missed?

The days did not roll around and disappear quite like he had initially believed they would. He found himself gazing up at the sky to attempt at determining the time, and it always seemed to be in the same position. The flare of light sending a golden hue across the land around him. the sight of it burned his eyes, causing them to ache with searing delight, so much so he found himself doing it several times a day.

That is not to say he was not enjoying himself. He started every morning with a dip in the lake. In his own lake. His own personal private reservoir. Initially, beginning this ritual with a nervous run from his home, wearing just a pair of boxers. Tentative, anxious, apprehensive to start. Dipping one body part in at a time until every hair was submerged before he would paddle about, letting the cold water refresh him, wake him, and clean him.

But now he was going in completely naked. Stalking from the open door of his cabin which he never shut, or never locked, and making his way barefoot towards the ridge of the water. He would dive in taking, no hesitation to fully douse himself in water. Allowing it to floor into his lungs, the water stinging against his eyes, tingling in his chest until he could not breathe before he resurfaced. Spluttering and spitting out all the water that had entered him.

Another close encounter with death that he liked to play.

It had been several days and not a single person had come remotely near to him or his own area. He was no longer concerned that someone may arrive out of the blue, out of nowhere. He was hidden, shielded by his own sheer desire to be invisible. A clandestine operation. Nobody could find him. he was sure of that.

Or was it that nobody wanted to come near him?

For a moment he considered if he would be or was being missed. He toyed with his own mind consciously, tantalisingly teasing the way his brain could be split into two, or if he was feeling particularly intrepid, possibly five minds. They all had unique voices, cultivated from his own imagination, and mashed together with a figurine from a film or television show he had binged on, back when he had a screen. The evil sounding, bad news breaking, maleficent creature of course had to be Gollum-esq, appearing short and bent over with ashy grey skin and built down to the bone. But he could not shake the sound of his voice being squeakier and more feminine than he had envisaged that creature to sound.

Was it that the sound of a female was a connotation to inconvenience or predicaments?

His everyday voice was echoed, the voice had a slight stutter, and always sounded sceptical and unsure of everything but it was always there. He relied on and trusted that voice the most, as it had been with him for the longest, it had been with him almost back when he first started to hear them. It was not the oldest voice though, there had been one before, one he still shuddered to think about, but this voice almost never resurfaced. And for that he was grateful.

His good news or positive, friendly, caring creature had the face blushed out by bright white light, like the sun or an angel. He could not see or picture a face behind the voice, but the sound of the voice was clear as day. Small bumps forced themselves up to his skin and rested there as he listened to the positive sound radiating between his ears. It was his best friend from home. His best friend whom he believed he loved like a brother. The voice was deep, yet charismatic and charming, with a northern twang running through every word, his body ached at the sound of his voice. He longed for his friend to be next to him. He could hear it so clearly; so much as though he was sitting right behind him that he would often turn around and check that he was still alone.

He always was.

He remained on his own, aside from the voices of course.

But they liked to come and go as they pleased. He had little control over where they went, or what they did, or what they said.

He sat on the bank of the lake, his feet dragged towards him, his knees tucked under his chin. His trousers billowed with the wind, letting the crisp air fill the loose linen and creep its way up his legs, getting confused and caught somewhere around his knees where the trousers tightened. His mind soon emptied with the distraction of a beetle walking in front of him.

It was funny that. How quickly his mind could be distracted and altered. One second, he was laughing with the five, or was it six minds, and the next he was lying face down on the grass, nose to nose with a shiny black and purple beetle. Watching every leg lift itself off the ground and plunder forwards. His mind blown away by the fact the beetle could take hours to move the same distance it took him to move in two minutes and fifteen seconds. The beetle disappeared into some long reeds, and he felt mean fishing it out again for the third time and so turned back around and this time dipped his feet into the vast lake in front of him for the second time today. The feeling of the wind caught him back again, as he watched it dance and ripple across the body of water, playing with it making it move and shake alongside. Nature was dancing in front of him, for him. Nobody else was here so who would it have been for, except for him?

It filled him with absolute pleasure that he was the only person in the world who could see the same sight, who was feeling this same feeling and who knew that every gasp of wind, every ripple of water and every movement from another creature was for his pleasure and his entertainment. He laughed to himself about why he had felt the need to provide his own entertainment when he was surrounded by it. He rocked forward and slid his legs in further, his trousers soaking up the water, pulling it out from the bed and absorbed it into him, he was part of the lake and he liked that. He lay back, resting his head on the grass and sighing deeply. Gazing up at the sky, it was greyer today than it had been on other days here, a thick blanket of clouds of grey, white, and blue covered the sky.

So, was he being missed?

Don't be daft, you know not a single person cared for you, not a single person will ever notice you have vanished. Nobody will care to notice; nobody will care to look. Nobody misses you.

Well, that was that then. The voice in his head had spoken. He knew he had to leave, and this confirmed that he was correct. He knew he was home, he felt more at home being alone in an open vast land than he ever had back in his old life. A small part of him longed for just a few things in his past life. He did not miss the attention, as he had been somewhat famous back at home. No, no not one of those virtual celebrities who possessed nor acquired any lifelong skills. He was famous because he was born with a talent that his father had harvested and put time and money into. He was famous because when he was a child and had little choice he was put into camps and trainings and courses to nurture his gift which left him with almost no choice but to carry out. He did not miss that aspect of life, he did not miss the fame, the hate, the cruelty. He didn't even like to think about it now or speak of it.

Why should he taint this new perfect life with past horrors?

He missed his mum somewhat, his dog very much, and his best friend more than he would like to admit. But most of all he missed his brother. They could have come with him, although had he mentioned that he was leaving and never coming back they may have tried to talk him out of it. Maybe…That was if they cared that he was leaving. He could never decide how they truly felt about him. It was near impossible trying to determine one's own feelings about someone else, let alone trying to decipher how they really felt about you.

He twisted a strand of his hair around his finger, observing the colours of gold and yellow wrapped so tightly his finger began to go red then white. He felt a droplet on his hand, settling into his palm and tracing its lines. He looked up, only to be received with three more small droplets landing on his face like a helicopter pad. He glanced down at the lake and saw a cascade of drips in the water, the splashes created mini sink holes and whirlpools and he was amazed at the beauty of it all. If more water entered this lake, where did it go to stop it overflowing? He vaguely recollected something in geography or basic science about evaporation and cloud formation, but he had never been too good at school.

Only sport or the art classes!

The rain picked up and was soon pouring vast drops down, the size of them almost hurt his bare skin and he decided it was a fair warning from the weather to retire himself into his cabin. He had barely spent any time in there since arriving and it seemed like an adequate opportunity.

Though he was not sure what to do with himself!

3. A Walk in the Moors

Several weeks had now passed. By this point time had run from him. He had now almost lost track of time completely. the date was a myth, the time was a guess, the day of the week was a conjecture at best.

At first, he had started writing down the days. Writing down what day it was, without the date alongside, accompanied with a thought or memory or dream he had experienced in his journal. A tatty, brown leather book he had carried with him. This was the only thing that had continued through both his lives, if he wished he could flick back and read excerpts from a year previously, he could detail, compare, analyse how different he wrote, how his emotions were parallel, what he had done that day that was so different to today. He never did compare and contrast, he wasn't sure if he neglected to read past notes due to him attempting to defy that last life, as to read from it would only embolden words he had felt true then but did not agree with now. Or he was omitting their passage due to a fear he may crave that he was breathing the same air he did then.

Friday 09.07 – the sky was dark this morning when I woke, I was not sure if it was still night or just a grey day. I hate those days. Those are the sort of days that keep you inside, which is never my wish. I still woke and went for a run around the lake. It reminded me of my runs at home, I realise I forgot my good trainers, and for a second, I missed running at home, old home, but then I remembered where I was and how this view was more scenic and how this life was better and freer. I made my lungs hurt by the run and by the cold, it was a good pain though. I think I will try and run every day.

Sunday 11.07 – I dreamt about being at a party, it was a sort of memory-dream, but everything was slightly off, déjà vu and jamais vu all at the same time. It was one of those parties I would not ordinarily have been invited to or gone to if it weren't for him…In the dream everyone loved my outfit, and complimented my unique taste and sense of style, while if it had been a party in real life, they would have whispered about me in the corner, like they used to. The dream was nice though, I wish it was a reality, I wish to attend a party with him again, but I know that will never be, and even if it was to be it would never be as I wished, I know it is quite the opposite in that world.

I would withstand it all to spend one more night with him.

There are few things I miss but he is definitely one of them, I wonder if he misses me too. Do you think I use the word miss too much? I shouldn't really be dwelling on the past when I have such a future ahead of me.

Tuesday 20.07 – Would it be cheating to get a takeaway in this life? I really feel like an Indian.

The daily entries became less and less frequent, they began to fade away and soon became once or twice a week instead of everyday. He found himself counting back to when he remembered writing them to work out the day, but he was sure he was wrong. It could be a Saturday or a Wednesday. They were all the same to him anyway. Part of him was mournful about aspects of his life, but it was closed so quickly and compartmentalised to the rear of his mind that it never had time to infest his brain. He never thought about it for long enough to become sad or to have any regrets. That was something he had always been good at. Compartmentalising …The voices in his mind were good at helping him close that box and file it right into a corner of his mind he could not reach. He was terrible at showing his emotions, he had them, but he found them displeasing and a nuisance and so felt that most of the time they should be shut up and discarded. He had no time for feelings, no time for emotions; everything was detached and separated by a thin layer of dust called distain. He was never sure if it was himself stopping him from having emotions, or if he was purely incapable of them. Part of him wished it was the latter.

This morning, however, he decided that today he would write down something in his book. He did not care what he wrote or if it even made sense, but he was determined to put something down. He wanted some memory of his time, something to look back on next year when he reopened the marred pages. He wanted something positive to say. His scratchy writing scrawled across the page.

Someday of the week – I wish I were an animal sometimes, I wish to live as freely as a bird, or a squirrel or a rabbit. Being an animal holds so many possibilities, limitless! Nothing tying you down or holding you back, I bet rabbits don't have to work or pay bills. No requirements for clothes or shoes, no expectations from family or the world even. I wish to do like they do. I think I was born into the wrong skin. I wish to metamorphose into something else.

He closed the book after doodling a small rabbit at the bottom of his page, cross hatching its ears and tail and beaming at it proudly. It was almost endearing.

Across his desk there was a glimmer of light, stretching its way over the faded wooden table, and over to his stomach. He was naked, as he usually was. Letting the warmth of the air draw sticky against his skin. The glimmer of sunlight touching his bare flesh.

The sun was inviting, and he smiled slightly. There was something about the weather that made you want to change your mood. He wanted to be outside, enveloping the sun into his hair and skin, he could hardly think of anything worse than sitting inside again and painting, or reading or writing. He changed into clothes, layering on a baggy old top which fell down to his thighs with a pair of long shorts clipping against his kneecaps. Alongside a scruffy cap which his best friend had given to him. It had the words "little steps" on it which had always confused him. But he liked how he was never sure what it was referring to. Was it the length of the steps? Was it goals? Was it a small ladder?

He began to pull on some long socks and his walking shoes when a thought fleetingly crossed his mind. The sort of thought he acted on before he thought too hard about it. This time he did not let it fall out of the other ear or get wrapped into the tornado rolling around in the back of his mind. He dragged the thought forward and held it in the forefront of his mind. Holding it on a poster stand. In fact, one of the voices in his head kindly read it out for him, off the piece of parchment paper strapped to some wood with the words written on with a feather and ink in the neatest of handwriting.

If you wish to live like an animal, you should. No clothes, no shoes, nothing.

He was quick to rule out wearing no clothes. As although he preferred to travel naked, that had always been within his own company, it was easier in the lake where he knew there was not a soul around, but out in the wild, in the moors where it was possible for others to encroach his space. Besides, he was sure his pale skin would crisp up under the sun and he was not willing to deal with that sort of pain later on in the day.

But it would be so very at one with nature to walk without shoes. He thought to Hobbits in the Lord of the Rings and how they walked treacherous lands with no shoes on. Across snowy landscapes, and rocky terrains, and across open fields, and into forests and rivers. If Bilbo Baggins could do it, why couldn't he?

Without another thought, he threw his shoes across the room, they toppled over his pile of clothes on the floor.

Must do a wash!

He made a mental note in his head as he stared at the boot lying amongst the mountain of his clothing.

Pulling off his socks he grabbed his book and a bottle of water and headed outside. Taking a second to feel the ground between his toes. He let the grass tickle his skin, and the soft mud envelops his heels. He dug his toenails into the turf and felt like mini spades were cutting their way through the undergrowth.

Luckily the rain had stopped a few days prior otherwise his feet would have become soggy quickly, forming the little wrinkles on each of his toes that you get from being in the bath for too long.

Instantly, he was aware of the incredible decision he had made. He felt enthralled and excited for his walk, setting no limit for its length or duration. He would walk until he felt his feet would fall off and then after a short read, he would head back in the exact same direction, so not to get lost.

He had not explored the area much; mainly he had stayed confined to his small section as without a map or a phone or anything really, he was concerned about not being able to find his way back.

And so, he set off, walking away from his cabin, away from his car, which by the way had too seen no use since his arrival several weeks ago, and was now covered in bird poo, however many weeks that may have been. He walked past the lake where he loved to swim and run around, and headed up, heading up towards a hill over the next valley. He walked without looking back, practically at a run he was so excited. Letting each new ground be exposed to his bare feet, each time giving his feet a minute to adjust before proceeding onwards, and upwards. He enjoyed the grass and mud more than he did stones or twigs, it was just basic knowledge that the softer, more squelchy ground was more satisfying on the soles of his feet than a rougher, craggier terrain. The sun climbed in the sky and was beating down on him, the intensity rising with every step he climbed up the hill. He glanced over his shoulder to see how far he had come. His house had disappeared, it was impossible to make out, hidden under a heavy cloudy canopy of trees.

Another feeling of excitement caught him. What if he couldn't find his way back? What if he had to sleep out in the open land? Now that would be at one with animals.

He glanced up ahead, adjusting his cap from the sun so he could make out the edge of the hill ahead. The grass was tumbling over in the wind, curling around and up, moving together in one motion. A shortened cut out path wound its way up the side of the hill. Worn down either purposefully or due to the sheer number of people who may have traced the same steps he was.

He thought about the different people or animals who may have taken the same steps as him. He wondered just how many, the proportion if you like, of those people who would have been wearing shoes.

Children running ahead and then stopping to watch their slow parents catch up behind them. Beads of sweat formed on his forehead under his cap.

Dogs off the lead would sniff across the grass, lifting their legs to urinate slightly to track their own scent whilst their owners whistle after them. He wiped the back of his forehead with his hand admiring the glistening liquid that he withdrew from it.

Elderly couples walking arm in arm together, celebrating decades of marriage together as they amble alongside the rolling hills. He stopped for a second, feeling his heart pounding in his ears, he had almost been running up the hill.

He was used to sweating, used to pushing himself to the limit, feeling his body ache and groan and begging him to stop. He liked that feeling, that his whole body was exhausted.

He turned towards the view, the crystal blue sky was framing the greenery, emulating a fake backdrop but with more character. He was surrounded by hills or varying green and grey, yellow, and auburn, the colours cascaded down the banks dotting across the landscape. There was not a single indication of human civilisation, not a single house or car, not a billow of smoke from a fire, not a single sound other than that of the wind.

He felt free.

Maybe a rabbit traced this path, maybe that's what left these little round droppings on the side of the grassy terrace. He thought about how his dog would have loved to sniff and chew away at some of that poo and how he'd scold him but let him do it anyhow.

He lifted his cap off to allow his long hair to breathe, the front was stuck to his forehead and his neck felt hot by its presence. He relieved his neck by pulling the loose strands away from it, they were wet and sticky, so he wound them around and around into a small bun which he fastened at the back of his head. It was a little tight and pulled at his forehead, but he readjusted the cap back onto his head, ignoring the sharp tug at his hairline.

Turning back towards the top of the hill he spotted someone coming down towards him. If he was breathing heavily before it was incomparable to now. The thumping in his chest and neck picked up and he felt frozen on the spot. It had been weeks, months since he had encountered another human. And the sight of one now filled him with absolute terror. His skin pricked; his body ran cold despite the sweat. His hands and legs quivering.

He braced himself, as the middle-aged man continued to walk towards him, no, he was making a beeline for him. He was coming for him he was coming to get him he was coming to drag him off kicking and screaming, back to his old life, back to his refined and lonely existence, the man was coming to take away his freedom. He was very aware of his quick breath, his heart racing in his chest, pounding in his head, his ears filled with blood. The man was coming closer and closer, but he tried not to panic he tried to ignore him watching him. The man had caught site of his bare feet and quickly looked him up and down.

'Mornin',' the man finally said, beaming away at him.

He stood motionless for a second, his breathing slowing as he realised, he might be safe after all.

'Good morning,' he responded, almost spluttering as he spoke.

He had not heard his voice in weeks, he had not uttered a peep whilst being alone and it surprised him how weak and pitiful it sounded. It was unpractised and shy, coarse, and reticent.

'Oh, I see, you're not from around here!' the man responded, his face red and jolly, his belly protruding over a thick brown belt with water strapped into it almost in the place where a gun was usually seen.

The man chucked as he spoke, touching his face, lifting up his safari hat which kept flopping down in front of his eyes.

He shook his head in response to the man, struggling to maintain his eye line, his face remaining blank and emotionless.

'Ere on holiday?' the man continued, taking the opportunity to look him up and down again, resting a little too long on his bare feet.

He sighed, shaking his head, and shuffling his feet from side to side, feeling nervous and conscious about them now. Covering one foot with the other, before swapping so they weren't exposed alone for too long. And this is why he hated humans and their civilisation. He felt ashamed. He felt a cold run of abasement filling its way through his body.

'I live here now, I moved here.' His voice was monotone but gaining some strength.

The man looked up, his face lit up with joy, his red cheeks practically bursting away from his face. They looked like red apples ready to be ripped away from his flesh, almost painful under his skin.

'Ah!' The man chortled. 'Lovely, whereabouts are you living then?'

He looked at him confused; he was not about to reveal his secret location to a complete stranger. Now, that would be stupid. He still was unaware if this man was after him, if he was luring him into a false sense of security in order to obtain this highly confidential information off him. He did almost feel like a spy with a secret, on a secret mission to maintain his privacy and his own secret life.

'Just a valley over,' he replied coyly, cocking his head in the opposite direction in which he came, trying to throw the man off his scent.

The man nodded, feeling apprehensive about the curtness of the conversation, the man looked as if he were about to move on, but he still did not, instead the man slowly began to look more and more concerned.

'Did you lose your shoes, Son?' the man asked carefully with a solemn yet empathetic face, his cheeks had dulled down in size but were still just as red.

'No,' he responded instantly and bluntly.

The man was taken aback by his candidness, he frowned briefly but only needed a second before he was smiling again.

'Okay then, it seems like you're doing well. So, enjoy!'

The man chuckled to himself, making his way past him, giving him one last glance over before carrying on his way, his arms swinging viscously as if propelling him forwards as he paced down the side of the hill. He watched after the man for a second before rubbing his feet and continuing up the hill in the opposite direction.

It was a close shave, but almost nice to interact with another human. Nice to utilise his vocal cords, get his mind whirring away thinking of how to be social, how to communicate. The memory of the man lasted a few seconds before he was distracted by something else, his mind flitting from one attraction to the next.

He wondered if he should write a book about the walks he created from his new home. A homage to his new life, so that he would never forget them. And the walk could be betwixt with whatever thoughts he had cultivated, or whatever the voices had spoken to him.

The voice which was deep and guttural and reminded him of some sort of goblin or devil living deep, deep under the earth, had been very vocal this morning. Talking to him about what life was like back home without him. And this voice made him certain he had made the right choice.

4. Nights

When it came to night, he would always dread it, he would hide in the cabin when the lights dimmed outside. The eerie silence falling across the wood. Every sound seemed to be accentuated when it was dark. The dimming of his visual sense seemed to alert his auditory sense. It set him on edge, it filled him with terror. And worse, it only further reiterated his loneliness.

The nights definitely were not as easy as the days. He did not scare easily but there was something about being alone in a foreign area that was still uneasy to him. There was still a childlike aspect within him where he needed the reassurance of safety, the knowing there was someone else to help him fight off whomever may come attacking.

Of course, he knew nobody would find him for miles, but he was not certain of this fact, and he wondered just how long it would take for a lunatic pick-axe murder to hack his or her way through the door and chop him into little pieces to scatter him across the forest.

He knew he was being preposterous, but he could not shake the nervous, unease and chattering of his teeth and hands. His palms and the backs of his legs collected sweat within them, a sticky, uncomfortable feeling which made him appear sickly and pale. His body shook in bed.

The fear was not helped by the noises surrounding his ears as he tried to close his eyes. The walls and ceiling did not seem as protected or thick as they appeared, every night a cacophony of sounds would radiate through the walls.

Rain fell on the ceiling and made him feel he was in a house made of tin, the powerful droplets shocking him as they reverberated across the room. Hammering down above him, he occasionally would seclude like a recluse under the duvet covers, covering his ears with the fabric and squeezing his eyes so tightly they hurt.

This night the usual tossing and turning was not helping. He sat up in bed, tired of reading. His eyes begged to be shut, their ache dragging his lids down, but he could not switch his mind off. It was running around for some reason, there was some tasks that desperately needed completing before it too could shut down.

His body was sleeping but his mind was wide awake and therefore he was wide awake. He lay, face up, eyes open, staring at the dark ceiling, counting the cracks and holes in the wood. The rain was echoing across the room, its slightly melodic, yet haunting sound drifting through him. He listened to it allowing it to render him peaceful.

The constant, steady and dependable patter lulled him into a fixed haze, drifting seamlessly through the sky, his eyes blurred by clouds, and it was not long before his mind had taken him away. He was no longer in the clouds, but he was running, he was running through a street, no he was running in a race, the race was on a street, people surrounding him. He was winning, of course, he was always the winner in his mind, and people were cheering his name. Rows and crowds of people filling every empty corner of the road, in blasts of colours and blurs of light as he eased passed them.

A marathon, he presumed.

And yet he felt delightfully full of air, he felt light as a feather as he glided across the path, his muscles not aching or begging to stop, in fact they felt rather energetic, the ground hot and burning under the sun, but he was not in a sweat, he was a comfortable clammy with enough moisture to keep his legs from chaffing but dry enough to maintain his hydration.

He was cheering himself on; his smile charismatic and characteristic, people were climbing on top of others, standing on chairs, crawling through legs just to get a snippet of him. The crowd screaming, calling out to him and—He made the mistake of moving on his bed and the vision left him, he was back in the dark, echoed room, the sound of the rain heavier than ever.

It was not so peaceful now.

He squeezed his eyes shut tightly again, wishing, and hoping to be transported somewhere else. Anywhere else!

Then he was, he was somewhere familiar and yet never felt more distant from it. The reassuring scent of chamomile and eucalyptus surged through him, the dull blue bed sheets with pillows scattered in disarray, the fuzzy grey carpet underneath his feet, he was wearing socks which was unusual for him now, but this was not his room.

There were posters of bands and footballers on the wall, something so garish for his parents he knew this was not in his house. He lay back on the bed, knowing full well this was not a memory but a fabrication of one, a fantasy. He was alone at first, taking in the Egyptian cotton white of the walls, contrasted to the Aztec curtains which were surely picked by a seven-year-old, the room seemed small, but it was well lived in.

Then the door swung open, and his friend was grinning, holding two cheese-toasties in his hands, the oil from the cheese dripping down his palm and his wrists. He immediately started to smile as well, feeling his cheeks fill with colour and becoming instantly conscious that he had been lying on his friend's bed. He edged to the corner of it, half hanging off it, gingerly taking the toastie from his friend.

He took a bite and could practically taste the warm, melted cheese all the way from his cabin in the woods. The burning sensation against his tongue, the rough burnt quality of the bread. He felt instantly warm, and then his friend put his hand around his back. The warmth intensified and he felt confused and lost, his emotions spiralling.

He took another bite but this time the cheese was hotter, he burnt his tongue and could no longer taste the tangy cheese, did not feel the coarseness of the bread, it went down his throat like a hard pebble, grating against his oesophagus as he tried to swallow the dry feeling within.

His friend retracted his arm and he realised he had been tensed, he had frozen up and seized in an upright position like a plank of wood. His whole body relaxed and soon he was spiralling away, heading out the door backwards, one hand holding the cheese toastie the other holding out for his friend, but there was no stopping him now. He backpedalled out the front door, down the road, across fields and rivers and ended up back in his bed in the cabin in the woods. He looked down and saw his empty hand, it still felt greasy from the toastie but there was nothing there.

He sighed and turned over, trying again to get to sleep. There would be no more dreams today.

5. Psychosis

He spent the next week sitting by the lake, in his favourite spot on the bank, watching the wind dance across the surface whistling a playful tune which made him want to dance alongside. But he was stretched out in front of him, one leg crossed underneath his bottom, the other reached out in front of him. Wearing just a pair of cotton cream trousers that were far too large for him and his hair tied back in a ponytail at the base of his head.

He had a large stretch of crumpled paper in front of him, half draped over his leg and the other turning in the wind as it rested gently on the grass. He had graduated from pencils earlier in the week and was now deeply pressing oils onto the page, allowing the colours to spread and spill, not bothered if they were running across in different directions or if the wrong colour merged with another creating a murky brown and a deep soulful grey.

He loved mistakes, he admired the way things could turn out so ugly, he liked the fresh hues that could be cultivated from an innocent flick of the wrist or drop of the hand.

It had been several hours since he last looked up and his neck was in agony, aching terribly. He wanted to keep going but this was the limitation of the human body.

He pushed the paper off his leg and unfolded the other from underneath him, his knee clicking and twinging after being fixed for so long under his weight. He stretched his legs out across the grass, his bare toes tickling each blade as they ran past it, allowing his nails to dig into the mud.

He rested his head back behind him, turning his neck gently to try and ease it out of its spasm.

He sighed, his eyes closing, the sun had disappeared a few days before hand, but the constant white sky was quite alluring. It was moodier, more dramatic and he too could reflect its atmosphere. He felt antipathy to pathetic fallacy, but today it seemed suitable. He loved the weather and the exciting stories it could tell. He loved to think about the impact it had on people.

Then his mind went spinning and the words started slipping from his mouth, reciting a story or a poem from his memory. He was desperate to hear the sound of his own voice, the words vibrating out through his throat and projecting across the water, sending his own ripples of noise. He was not speaking to anyone, and yet he was telling the story as if the whole world was listening.

'There is something about the sky, in particular, and how its slight slips and changes can depict a mood, a scenario, and a series of events. The slight glimpse of sunlight in Britain causes a cascade of Britons to take to the streets and parks in strappy tops and short shorts which let their arse cheeks hang out of them. They take to the parks to sit in the barely warm sun and drink beers and ciders pretending it is already summer when it is only in fact April, the ground temperature barely being above 10 and yet there they persist, the stubbornness of the English is something which must be admired. Contrary to this the gloominess of a foggy day, where the world is grey, buildings are numb and dull, the thick fog hangs in the air blending into the ground making everything feel like it's trapped in its muggy abyss. This sort of weather keeps people in doors, the sort of weather where you should go for a run or a walk, but you cannot be bothered, and it is deceivingly warm due to the mugginess so a speedy walk can make sweat collect under your armpits and down your back whilst your hands and feet are fucking freezing. But the cold isn't always hated, the cold in winter where the weather randomly decides it's time to snow and the world becomes a magical place, the sounds of traffic and people are muffled by the squelch of soggy snow and creaking of footsteps in the crisp freshly fallen blanket. The lining of silvery white which sits on every branch of a tree no matter how narrow will never fail to amaze me, its simple elegance is captivating and yet can never be adequately immersed in a single photograph. The other amazing thing about the British is their fascination with snow, how even if it is the smallest, dampest and most pathetic snowfall in the country you'll know about it because someone will have posted it, on their story, on their feed, on twitter, on TikTok, the myriad of platforms will make you aware, and sometimes jealous, that somewhere in the country the weather is different from where you currently sit, or stand, or lay, I don't know how you are hearing this. But it will forever amaze me how the weather is such a vitally important indicator of the world, and I cannot quite depict it in words, but it is my favourite thing to describe, and draw and write. How the brightness of the blue sky can make at least ten people a day exclaim "look at how blue the sky is!" or the number of times a beautiful sunset will be captured and not done justice on an iPhone camera. But also, how rain is associated with sadness and its pathetic fallacy with break-ups and misery when in fact if you are prepared for it, and prepared to get wet it can be an exhilarating feeling to be out in.'

He froze, panting as if he had spoken all in one breath, the words tumbling with a rhythm. He was still lying flat down on the grass, glancing around as if he were waiting for the crowd who must have been listening to him to respond. The eerie silence withheld; the distant sound of a pigeon hooted gently.

'But the weather is also the perfect trigger for a memory, trigger memories. And for me, still, I associate the bright blazing, burning sun with one memory that I would quite like to erase,' he continued grimly. But he was finished now, he had dampened his own damp mood and was now lifting himself off the grass. He was done with drawing for today, done with painting, he was done with the day.

There were times, often similar to that morning, he could force himself to be transported to another world. He could lie on his bed, or did the transportation start before he lay down? He could never remember. He liked to think he was in control of himself, when in fact it was probably the voices who decided what he did.

Anyhow, somehow, he would be lying on his bed, his mind spinning. Psychedelic streams of colour, bright reds, deep purples, royal blues, greens, yellows, every colour you could possibly imagine would roll out in front of him as he travelled through time to something better. Some place where he could be exactly who he wanted to be. It had been a skill he had perfectly honed over the last six years, the ability to transform oneself into a grandiose version of themselves.

He was everything he wanted to be.

But of course, it was all his choice, he believed.

He was able to walk the streets of home, his brother behind him talking some rubbish about how if he did a different kick roll on a video game, he would complete an incomplete level. He had never been interested in video games, but he enjoyed hearing his brother be so passionate about them.

He could his brother's voice so clearly; he could make out his face so perfectly and then he could come to touch it and it would disappear. It would vanish like a bubble popped and he would be back where he started, his body in a slightly shifted position, often drooling.

He could always get it to come back though, but it was never the same, he just now knew not to approach it just in case he lost it one day for good.

He had never spoken to anybody about his travels, he had never mentioned to his parents that he sort of believed his brother would come and see him from time to time that he would be the most lifelike form and he could talk and move and laugh. He did not think to mention how he could hear others speaking to him, or hear them telling him to do things, how they would guide him along. For the voices were his friends, he didn't think there was anything wrong with them.

Most of the time they were just there for a chat, they hardly ever told him something mean or offensive, they mainly just wanted to check in and tell him something he may have missed.

Was there really so much wrong about that?

People can hear their own voice in their head, or at least most people can, so he felt there was nothing wrong with the sound of a few other, now familiar voices accompanying his own. Although his own voice was more of a mute now, he had been stunned to silence by the opinions of his friends.

There had only been one time where he had considered telling someone about his voices or the things he could see. He thought about telling his best friend.

It had been after a game you see, and he had been hearing salacious things whispered into his ear about the opponent, things he never would have dreamed of thinking, the most terrible thoughts that he did not imagine possible. He had found it disturbing and distracting and partly disgusting. The words were dripping out of his ear like lava from a burning mouth, singeing his cheek as they trickled down with every breath.

It had scared him how aggressive they had gotten with him and the terrible things they had been saying felt so far out of his mind he knew this voice was not part of him. He had not played well that day, missing several opportunities and his team had let him know it, voicing their own mean and harsh opinions which too had impacted him.

He only failed to disclose this incident to his friend as this was the first day his friend too had said he had let him down today. His friend had admitted with sad eyes and a lost, vacant expression that he was not on form that day and it had impacted them all.

That feeling of letting down his friend was more painful than the burning voices within his ear, the scorched feeling against his cheek. His stomach was like a burrowed animal and so he held his tongue, he did not want to retaliate with some ridiculous excuse *such as the voices in my head told me to, or distracted me.*

He cried that evening and decided not to tell anybody about what he could hear, but also not to let them impact him again. He shouted at the voices that night, in his own voice, they had only been united for a couple of years at this point so he was tentative to tell them off, for fear of what they may do to him. So, he banned them from talking during a match, he could hardly afford the distraction, the disappointment from others, he could not bear to see that face on his friend again.

In the end of a psychedelic spin, he always came back to normal reality, usually unwillingly, and he was sitting under a table or by a road giggling to him.

6. Trapped within Four Walls

It was evening all too soon every day, and each day he regretted not spending it completely outside. If it was windy, or cold, or wet, or warm he would had rather have been outside until he could barely make out his own hand in front of him.

There was so much more to see and do outside than there was boxed within four walls. It was so restrictive being inside and being in the cabin just reminded him that he was in fact alone, no matter how many times he tried to convince himself he felt better now. It reminded him that, despite feeling more reassured about where he was, he was still very much alone, and he had nobody to talk to. And what was worse was that being alone, and inside made him think about the past, it made him remember things he never wanted to. Things he had worked for years now to shut down and keep closed in the back of his mind.

He had learnt to excel at closing things away. As soon as they occurred, they would be filed into his brain, sorted into a pleasant or distraught memory, and then compacted away into small, chained chests. Locked and hidden, unobtainable. Only resurfacing when he was jolted by imagery.

After being in the cabin, in the lost cabin in the woods, it felt like a ticking time bomb for one chest in particular. The feeling of being cornered, captured, kept hostage by walls he could not escape.

As the evenings drew in, so too did the timer on the bomb expired, and the memories splattered out across his mind.

Being encased within four walls reminded him of being trapped in locker rooms, the last place he would want to be, it reminded him of the smell of sweaty feet and choking deodorant. It reminded him of merciless teasing and joking, even if he had played incredibly and scored a hat trick and given two assists, somehow those days seemed to be worse.

Jealousy was such an ugly trait to possess. He remembered that specific day where, he had been rated a 10/10 by both Sky Sports and BBC sport, at the absolute peak of his short career. Feeling happy for once, feeling content with his achievements. His coach liked to read off everyone's rating win or lose so individuals were singled out for playing the worst in the team. And on this day, he remembered dirty items of clothing being flung at his head. Along with words he did not wish to remember.

Being inside reminded him of items of his own clothing being stolen and hidden high up on top of places he could not reach. It reminded him of communal showers and sharing towels and body washes. The sickening smell of damp shoes and soiled underwear. It reminded him of mocking tones and aggressive threats. It reminded him of coming home feeling embarrassed, ashamed, and partly terrified even when he had played well. He had felt permanently dejected, constantly on the edge of tears. Forever terrified of what the day would bring when he was poised inside, trapped within four walls.

But it was all forgotten the moment he stepped outside, the teasing and torturing which was relentless behind closed doors was all vanquished the moment he stepped onto a grassy green and started to kick a ball around. It was like everyone was tricked into a trance where they could not help but watch the skill he had and the ball at his feet like an extension of his body. Left foot, right foot it was all the same, he had been gifted with the magic touch and yet taking him off the pitch and putting him back inside it made him the most hated person in any room.

He had a gift.

Or so everyone would tell him.

A gift that made people stop and watch him. A gift that made those people who teased him shut up and start praising him instead. This gift was found by a scout when he was nine years old and since that day, he had sold his life, personality, and individualism away. From that moment, there was not one day which passed without him touching a ball with his feet or being ordered to touch a ball with his feet.

He was pushed around, forced to the limit and to the point of tears, to the point of vomiting, to the point where he was lying face down in his bed screaming into his cushion.

He enjoyed it at first; he enjoyed the work, the outdoors, and the fun. He enjoyed being picked first for every game, he enjoyed the praise at first and he enjoyed playing for his country, scoring for his country, playing for his childhood favourite team.

But it slowly became resentment, the praise turned sour and jealous and bitter, the time away from everything else, the loneliness that came with it as nobody was his friend off the pitch.

He was admired by hundreds but also hated and threated by thousands. He earned money, lots of money, but he also was robbed, beaten and abused every day.

The ball he had brought along with him had remained outside, still resting by the base of the tree. The butterfly had gone and not returned.

It seemed arbitrary now, in his new life, kicking a ball around, still feeling a slight thrill from kicking it up and stopping it dead on the ground, twirling it around his feet and finishing it beautifully to hit any target he liked. How could something so simple to him captivate the minds and souls and lives of so, so many individuals.

He knew people whose livelihoods revolved around football, they spent money on memberships and tickets and shirts and signed posters and events. They wasted tears on lost games and got aggressive with others but also felt elation and mocking when they won.

And yet it just came so easily to him, it was second nature to his feet. He passed the ball between his two feet, gracefully gliding it from the ground, to the air, to his chest, and his knees and back to his feet again.

All in one swift, fluid movement!

He smiled coyly to himself as he kicked the ball off into the distance, watching it turn away from him and roll down a hill into a bush.

His smile soon faded as his memory turned to the bad times. He had been selected for the senior squad at his local premier league team at seventeen years, starting and playing most games for them by the time he hit his eighteenth birthday. Since then, he was a regular, a star player, requested by many other clubs but he stayed where he was to remain close to home, close to his parents, and to stay loyal to his team and the fans. Though this did not stop the cascade of messages of hate and aggression he got from neighbouring teams and rival clubs who wanted to sign him instead.

He was eighteen, the first time he had ever step foot in a club. A nightclub he had been dragged to by his team. By his friend mostly. The image of the darkened room, the multicoloured strobe lighting forever ingrained in his mind. He remembered the sticky floor and the way he could feel the bass of the music deep within his body. Feeling it in his throat, his chest, his knees. The sound pulsated through his frame, undulating from his toes to his eyes.

He remembered drenched bodies pressed up against his own. Prying eyes as he was led through the crowd to a private box. Lined with girls, all kinds of women. Pressing themselves against our signed off section in the darkened corner of the room.

He recollected not being able to breathe, feeling short of breath in the suffocating heat of the room, the feeling of artificial smoke squeezing at his lungs. Choking him into a spluttering heap, one hand pressed against the wall for support. Bent over, heaving and hacking until he saw blood.

He recalled declining every drink offered his way. Not one mention of a spirit or beer was tempting. He was tired of shaking his head, tired of the no thank yous, exhausted from explaining why he did not want to consume any alcohol at all. It was taxing watching the bewildered faced frown and then turn away from him for the hundredth time the same night.

One by one his teammates left the fenced off section, disappearing into the crowd. Usually linked arms with one of the girls who had appealed. He remained firmly seated, legs crossed over one another, tightly pressed into one corner of the plush black cushioned chairs. Attempting his hardest to be enveloped by them.

That was until his friend was the one to take his arm. Leading him away from the chairs. Onto the sticky floor, surrounded by hundreds of other sweat riddled figures, blending and blurred with their movements. He felt dizzy just being in the centre of it.

But for a moment, for a second he had fun. He danced, he moved, he laughed, he smiled.

The moment passed as quickly as it came. He realised that hands were on him. Hands he did not approve of and did not recognise. His friend whisked away by the girlfriend. He was alone, surrounded by indistinguishable faces and so many hands. They touched him all over. Everywhere. Hands running along his chest, his back, his legs, his bottom.

His body freezing at the touch, shuddering at the dislike, the loathing he felt from the unwanted hands across his body. But he said nothing. He let them touch him. Let them exploit his body, believing it was expected. Presuming it was something he was to enjoy and accept.

He felt dirty after.

Leaving the club alone.

Not actually having anything but hands on his body but that had been enough. It had not been what he had wanted. It had been forced upon him all the same.

He was sat on the ball now. Crushing it underneath his weight. Letting the shape bend with his body. His eyes shut, his heart pounding. He felt his face was burning hot. He hated that memory.

He hated every encounter with strangers.

Because each time they treated him like they knew him, like they possessed him.

He remembered walking home from training at just nineteen years old, after succeeding in a series of starts for his premier league team. He could not yet drive but he could represent his club and country. He remembered feeling joyous about his achievements, goals, assists, vital passes, he was exceeding above and beyond what anyone thought he would and at such a young age as well he was envied by other clubs, idolised by children and hated by rivals.

On this particular day, it was turning dark after a five o-clock finish in late winter. He had to walk today due to his parents unable to pick him up, he was in the midst of driving lessons. Desperate to pass quickly to try out the car that had already been purchased for him. He was walking along, his boots slung over one shoulder, his clothes crumpled into a bag hanging from his back when he was cornered into an alleyway by four men with their hoods up and masks over their faces. None of them even spoke, none of them tried to reason with him. Before he even realised it, he was being hit. He was robbed, beaten, and left bleeding on the side of a main road. People had walked past and nervously noticed him down the alley, they saw his pleading eyes and heard his cries and yet they had done nothing. He had been alone in an ambush. He would never know if the men knew who he was or just identified him as an easy target.

He had been.

He always did and always would blame it on his job.

He had been terrorised for his job, his skills, his talent and he had been punished for just living and being good at what he did.

The worst part of being tormented was never the abuse he had received from fans; he expected it. It was from those he knew that hurt the most, it was more that it only started after a certain point.

He used to be friends with all those boys, he used to have a close relationship with his team, with the fans, with his family.

He used to be able to go out to social events, or team dinners, or sing karaoke in front of strangers and make a fool of himself. He never wanted to disappear into the cushion of a club sofa before.

And then one day, that particular one day, everything changed, and he became a whole new person. Those abilities stripped from him, and he felt awkward and alone and liked to spend time in his room rather than with his friends. He still enjoyed the football of course, he enjoyed the satisfaction and the competitiveness of it, but like everything else, its attraction faded away and he was left wanting to run away.

Wanting to hide.

Wanting to leave town and live as a recluse in a lost cabin in the woods.

He wanted to do anything to escape being trapped in four walls.

7. Him

Social media had been a downfall for him, and he was not alone in that aspect. He was one of those who would scroll through thousands of comments and messages and posts about himself. He abused himself, tortured himself by allowing himself to be impacted by them. He let them wound him, he let them leave a scar across his body, a puncture in his skin and he let their words eat away at his flesh until he was left skinless. His organs hanging outside of his body, embedded with the necrosis it left behind.

It was his own form of self-flagellation, he would read just enough until he was left bloody and teary in the corner of his room, shielding himself from the dangers of the electronic world. His hands shaking and wringing with sweat that his phone would slip from his hand and reverberate along the floor.

It became so bad at one point that it was noticeable, but only to one person. To his friend. His best friend.

His friend had noticed the sudden change, the shaky, pale faced shadow of a person he had become, who would slink into the changing room. Barely able to control the cold sweats he now permanently lived with. He would hover in his seat, scarcely able to utter a word through his colourless lips. It was obvious in some regards; however, his friend was the only one brave enough to confront it. The only one who cared enough. His friend decided it was time to delete all his accounts, mute the world from his device and stop him from searching his name. His friend monitored him, daily. Checking in, calling, texting, dropping by just to talk. For weeks, months, he would receive contact, attention, and solicitousness from his friend.

His friend pulled him out from the dark corner where he was convulsing and perspiry and resurrected him, giving him social media CPR as it were.

It was not possible for a single day to amble by where he did not reminisce being with his friend. He found refreshing pleasure in often lying in bed wondering what his friend was up to at that moment. What his friend may be thinking of, or who his friend was talking to at training, if his friend was missing him.

Typically, since that day, he was the sort of person that people usually avoided spending time with. Avoided being seen with if they could, especially outside of his work.

It has been made clear that he was talented, nobody could deny him that, but outside of a football environment he was a seemingly strange being.

The sort of person who dressed in eccentric colours and patterns, never matching them in what is deemed fashionable.

He cultivated his own style, unique and independent of thought and trends. He found different things funny, studying conversations far too hard to discover when the correct time to laugh was. He enjoyed discussing topics that most others he spent time with did not even know about. Things they had never even heard of and had absolutely no interest in learning about.

He liked the arts, which in itself was not abnormal, but he was surrounded by others who did not care for reading, writing, and drawing as much as he did.

They could not appreciate the fine lines behind a sketch. The levels of intricate detail you could appreciate from one brush stroke or from one simple prose. He could consider the background work that went into the profession he was in, the level of time and detail that went into every promo of a new shirt, or a new boot. The sort of detail that was completely overlooked and unrewarded.

He was what people called different.

Which meant he was usually avoided and left alone at all costs, people respected his space and avoided eye contact that could spark a conversation they did not want to start. Rarely were conversations brought to him, and slowly after time he stopped commencing them himself. And the loneliness dragged.

That was for all except one.

All aside from his friend, his best friend he liked to believe.

His friend never seemed to appear like it was a burden to spend time with him, he never criticised his outfits, in fact his friend often stated how much he admired his sense of style. His friend never looked displeased with his topic of conversation, their debates would be lively and often raucous and his friend liked spending time with him.

His friend would invite him out all the time, out to the pub, to the cinema, out to play football for fun instead of for money, he would invite him around to his house, drive him around in his car and take him out for meals.

He saw his friend every day, every day for as long as he had known him, which was around eight years now. There was a connection from the offset, back when he liked socialising, and they were instant friends, two boys cut from the same cloth. With similar families and intense, fearful childhoods they bonded. His friend took a liking to his brother, taking his brother in as a sibling of his own. The three of them spending hours together. Wasting away time watching crap television and competing in videogames.

Then the change came, and he became more secluded, more awkward, and shyer, but his friend did not change at all. They still continued to do the same things as if nothing had changed, as if nothing was now missing. His friend never treated him different because of what happened, and his friend only brought up the conversation if it had been sparked by himself.

Those moments were the only periods where he felt that it had never happened. When time was spent with his friend. In fact, time suspended, he could never feel it pass the way he did normally. It was just him and his friend, normal. Something he could depend on, rely on, something constant. Something protective.

He missed his friend very much; his voice was still abundantly clear in his mind, the calming, kind voice which spoke to him almost daily. It echoed around his mind, with its northern ring, and charming charismatic laugh. The only sound that could instant fill him with joy, with his own laughter. It filled him with peace.

But it was not the same as having the real person in front of him. He missed hearing his friends' balanced views about life, he ached thinking of their lively debates, and admiring his funny anecdotes. He missed how his friend made him feel, because he did make him feel so very good inside.

He thought often about telling his friend what he had done, about telling his friend where he had gone and why he had done it! He owed his friend a lot of his time and respect, but did he owe him this?

Did he owe him his new life, his freedom?

They had once been out for a meal in an Old Italian deli, eating at what could be deemed as a bar. Sharing plates of warmly baked focaccia, deep green stuffed olives lathered in oil, thick freshly cut pasta with lemon and thyme and mountains of parmesan, tiramisu after tiramisu.

Of course, this was only on their time off, they would never dare to eat like that during a season. They spent hours together, wasting their time away whilst they were not training, or spending time with their families, all of those spare moments were spent together. Often not even speaking, they could sit for hours in silence.

His friend liked his drawings, often asking what he had been working on and making kind, balanced remarks on the work he showed.

His friend was talented at music and played several instruments for him, showing off in a considered and modest way. There was something so individual and unseen in his friend, a rare quality you find in a hidden gem of a person.

The greatest sort of friendship where they both hid their desires and passions from the rest of the world, leaving it solely exposed for one another.

On the football pitch he had played in the centre, his friend at the front and they had often succeeded in assisting the other in goals. They were a pair, a team, a duo. His friend was one of the only people he knew who had met his entire family, and who was loved by his entire family. And who was loved by his entire family.

Another older brother to his own brother, another, often preferred son to his parents. His best, and only friend in the whole world. He was a charmer, a delight, a warm natured, kind-hearted soul. A lightness in the dark, a flower in a desolate field, the breath of fresh air after a floor.

He wished more than anything that he could tell his friend everything, he wanted to tell him so badly.

But where to even begin?

8. A Homage to Death

This morning I thought I would write about something different in my diary; it was something that I have been wondering about for a while and today in particular I sat and pondered about what death would look like if he were a person, or she, or they in fact. I wondered how death would be represented if they took on a human form, as a lifelike specimen who walked and breathed and spoke. But if you think of death as a person like me, it does become less terrifying. It becomes more mundane, he has a job just like everyone else, it is just his is far more morbid.

Often, people portray death as a huge, cloaked in drapes of black fabric. A figure that would make you shiver on the warmest days, a figure who you'd glance twice at due to their chilling disposition. They would be tall in stature and hunched over and so not truly portraying their great vastness, furthermore instilling fear in everyone.

In my opinion, death is someone not to be afraid of. Death is someone to expect, at all times, or likewise not expect at any point. You can never be sure or tell when he, she or they are around the corner. Death sits at the side of every room waiting for a poor soul to be swallowed up into the afterlife, they can be suspecting, knowing, begging, or surprised by death as they are greeted by him, her or they and can walk alongside death like a friend or be dragged kicking and screaming by the ankles.

But death is not a cloaked, dark figure, death is someone simple, a simple teenager who made a mistake, a simple mother who did not express the pains in her body before it was too late, a simple man who forgot to check his car fully that morning, an innocent child who did not know what had hit him. Death embodies mothers, fathers, children, siblings, cousins, friends. Death is within everyone and no one all at once.

If I were death for a day, I think I would see if anyone's time was drawing to a close, and I'd give them an extra day to spend with their family, with their friends. I'd allow them just one more goodbye, as sometimes they don't know when goodbye should be said.

For instance, someone you see every few days as a staple, someone close, someone so consistent you do not think it is important to even say goodbye because you know you'll see them in a few days. Let's say you see that person one Sunday, you spend an incredible, fun, exhilarating day alongside them, just like you always do. Then at the point you'd usually hug and say farewell, you're distracted, or they're own the phone to somebody else, so you wave from the distance, or you fail to gesture or say anything at all and think to yourself you'll get to them next time. You fail to give them that final goodbye as the next day, unknowing and unsuspectingly, they are stolen from the world. They are seized by death and dragged away without the chance to say their own goodbyes, their own thank yous, their own I love yous, they are gone.

Never to be seen or spoken to again.

It is hard when someone leaves like this because of the shock of it all, the shock that they are no longer there, there is no physical form of them, they do not exist anymore, merely their memory remains. The abrupt, unforeseen aspect of it makes it just that little bit more difficult. The body you once memorised, the shape and feel of a hug. The warmth of their skin, the smell of their clothes. Things that all eventually fade.

That figure is something you can no longer speak to, so you can never say the things you should have told them every day but thought it was too trivial or too embarrassing to admit the impact they had on your life.

And then, it is too late for anything.

You never got to tell them how much you appreciate them and their presence in your life, you did not get to tell them that you would not be the person you are today without their influence on your life, you didn't get to say that now you will embody a part of them that you most admire because you know that it is a trait to live by. The physical, emotional communication is taken from your grasp and stripped from your heart.

And sometimes, you did not get the chance to speak freely because you were unaware of how you felt until it was all too late. Although I hate the saying 'you do not know what you have until it is gone', it is times like these when I can appreciate the sentiment.

That is hard, that is painful, that is difficult to imagine or think or talk about. But what I believe is harder is the thought of what could have been. All the memories they will now not be there for, all of the stories they will be missed out of or miss hearing and enjoying. The people they won't meet who are important to you, the huge chunk of your life that you would share with them is now left empty.

I do not like to think about how new memories will be made and they won't be a part of them. I do not like to think that I could be happy without them, or I could laugh and reminisce without them by my side.

It seems strange to consider, but I despised when the new year came around because not only did it feel like a new start without him, but it felt like I was leaving him behind, leaving him in the last year. He would never progress to the New Year, he stayed frozen in the year that just passed, he would remain there, and I would move further away from him.

It is painful even to think about now. But I am not afraid of death as I know he, she or they will come for me one day. They could come today, or in two years, or when I am old and decrepit. They will come, and still I will not be afraid then either. I just hope that when death does come for me, I've said all of my goodbyes, all of my thank yous, and all of my 'I love yous'.

Though, if I am still here, in my cabin, it may be too late for that already.

Nobody really ever talks about death. There's no sort of lesson at school where you're sat down and told that eventually everyone will die, because I guess we all know that. But we never get told that everyone around us will also die and that there is no way of predicting when or how that will be. And worse than that, we do not get told what to do, or how to act when those around us die.

There is no way of getting over it, it affects each person differently, and you will have to find your own way to recover and move on. They also never tell you that the kind of death has an impact on you, yes, all death is terrible and a tragedy, but a sudden death compared to a long deteriorating one differs in the fact I have already mentioned, the goodbye.

They do not tell you that the way a person dies will also alter your reaction, for a long death gives you time to come to terms with it, a sudden death can leave you questioning why for years, maybe forever. Questioning whether there was anything you could have done differently to prevent it.

There is no way of getting over it, there is no magic potion to drink, no song you can sing, no amount of trying to forget or conversely trying to remember all of the good times that allows you to get over it.

For you never truly get over it, not really, I do not think I will ever get over it.

Not fully.

It is something that lives within me forever, and it will be with me forever. I cannot change how I feel about it now nor could I five years ago and I doubt I'll feel much different in the next five.

Nothing makes it easy, it is always hard, always painful, always scarring. The feeling never goes, sometimes it hides in the corner and lets you laugh, lets you smile, lets you remember what life like was before, but you know by the end of the day, or even the next day it will be back and often stronger than before. The sickening grief and guilt, winding you, knocking you over, making you remember even more painfully.

9. Time

It had been just under four months since he had left. And part of him felt a little anguish that nobody had found him yet. Then when he felt like that, he pinched himself until he drew blood. The point of being here had not been to be found, it was to never be found.

The voices in his head had almost doubled since he had arrived. Making sure he was never left alone long with his own mind. His own voice that he could faintly hear in the background of all their noise. It was becoming more and more difficult to make out what he was saying from what they were all saying.

They had such a force, such an impact on him. What he did, how he felt, what he said aloud. Most of that was dictated by another voice. Any other voice, he was never picky about which he listened to.

Not anymore.

Time had passed so incredibly slowly and quickly all at once.

Part of him could not believe it had been so long since he had driven away that morning. And the other part felt like it should have already been a year, if not two.

It was uncomfortable, settling the two sides of his body apart. The voices could not decide which side to take. But most of them concluded that he had done the right thing. He should have left and even if it were a mistake, it was too late now to change his mind. Too embarrassing to head back and correct the mistake he had made.

He watched the timer on the ticking clock go round. Counting the seconds at the same time. Watching time pass ever so slowly. It felt like each second dragged out a little longer.

It reminded him so painfully of hospital waiting rooms. Watching the dial of the seconds hand tick round the face ever so slowly.

He was waiting for his brownies in the oven to cook. It had been the first time he had actually used the oven and opened it to a nasty smell of charred leftover food. It had only taken him ten minutes to wipe it down clean, almost looking new again but the grease on the door was particularly difficult to shift.

The scent of the brownies now wafted around the cabin. Warming and chocolatey it filled the small space with a delightful odour.

Now all he could do was watch the timer go down. For fear he would get so distracted by something else, as he tended to do, and forget about the baked goods in the oven. Before they too would become a scorched heap in the base of the oven. He could not bear to clean it once again.

Distraction always got the better of him. Within a moment he was taking his cleaning products around the rest of the cabin. Stripping his bed of their sheets and covers, wrapping them into a ball and throwing them towards the door of the cabin. He would wash them in the lake later.

He ran a cloth and cleaner along the dusty windowsill next to his bed, across from the kitchen, in the bathroom. Disgusted by the line of dirt that pulled up along the cloth as he lifted it to observe.

Throwing the cloth away immediately he continued on in the bathroom, scrubbing away at the shower, the sink, the toilet.

A sweat formed along his hairline, pooling in his back and sliding down the centre, falling into his underwear.

His pants suddenly felt to hot, too restrictive. His genitals warm and itching in his boxers. The sweat collecting in the crack between his buttocks.

He stripped, down to just his socks. Walking around the cabin completely naked.

The thought did not even cross his mind. Being naked was so comfortable now he knew it would be preferential.

He washed his hands. Done with cleaning now. He left the box of cleaning products in the centre of the room. The dirty cloths strewn along the floor.

His bedsheets still in a heap pressed against the door. He took them out, carrying them down in just his socks to the lake. Throwing them in without a second thought.

The sheets began to float away from him, drifting out in the water.

He stood and watched, hands on his hips. Watching the spiral of white linen separate and float apart, separating across the body of water.

The beeping of the oven broke his trance. He ran back into the cabin. Flinging the door of the oven open and sticking his hands in to pull out the ceramic tray of melting rich chocolate.

His hands were bare, the tray burning hot. He forgot for a second. Dropping the tray directly on the floor.

It shattered instantly. White ceramic shrapnel breaking off and splintering the skin around his ankles. His skin splitting easily from the shards. They shone for a second bright red before the blood started to trickle down his legs. Collecting on the floor in a puddle. His feet submerged in it.

And all he could do was watch. Observe the blood pooling around his feet. Remark on the fresh burning hot brownies now sticking to the floor of the cabin.

He looked to his hands. The burn barely hurt. His hands glowed red and white. Their indentations seared off completely. They were unrecognisable. Blisters forming on them already.

But he felt nothing. Nothing on his hands, nothing around his ankles. Nothing from the loss of the food he had just made. It did not hurt; it did not send waves of achy pain up his arms.

In fact, it was as if nothing had touched him at all.

Nothing hurt him anymore.

It almost felt like he was a floating. He was not living a real life. Almost not living at all. He found a disengagement towards living.

A severing of his body from his life. He was not a real person any longer.

10. That Terrible Day

I think his detachment from life and his interest and enticement by death began years ago when his little brother had died. It had been a complete shock. A freak death, from a seemingly healthy and innocent young person.

I guess you could say he had never recovered. Although he never spoke about it, not to his parents, not to his friends, not even to the voices, not to anyone.

He held it inside of him until he would randomly burst and leave tears all over the floor, leaving a fresh scar on his skin, leaving a mess to clean up, and every time after allowing himself to cry he would regret his actions and promise not to let it happen again.

And it would not happen for even a longer time, but it always came back. But even in those cases it would be confined to his bedroom, and nobody would suspect a thing had occurred. His parents had not been concerned that he had not cried at the funeral, he had not cried when they cremated his body, he had not cried when they scattered his ashes. He kept it all in and waited until he was alone to cry himself to sleep every night for months.

He can distinctly remember the day and can replay it like a cassette tape in his head if he ever wished. A different kind of memory from all of the others, so ingrained that he could recite what occurred second by second, detailing down to the colour socks he had been wearing, and the mug he used for his tea with breakfast in the morning.

It was still a painful memory for him, but he was so used to watching the characters play out in his head that it was almost as if he was watching strangers, actors on a screen, it did not impact him personally. He rarely cried now, it was but five years ago and he had almost made himself numb by the memory of it.

He had left the house for school that morning, he had eaten breakfast with his brother at the kitchen table, cornflakes in a bowl with a green M&M face on the front and his tea in his dad's Bristol City football mug.

He had always had an excellent, close relationship with his brother and that morning they had been debating who would be better at rugby. Being brought up in a strictly football household it was a debate they liked to have. His brother was by far more muscular, and would have made a good prop or so, but he was taller and more agile, he was quick on his feet and small enough sideways to slip through players, he could have been a fly half or something. It was four weeks following his seventeenth birthday and there were still balloons scattered across the floor shrivelled into a quarter of the size, their dog still fascinated by them so they would take it in turns to kick the balloons at the dog and scare him into the next room. Giggling themselves into frenzy at the yelps their puppy would make in response.

He was only going to school today for the morning, and there was a certain excitement about those days where he got pulled out at lunch to go to football training. Something smooth and interesting about him and he knew that his peers would speak about him after his exit. His brother was doing the opposite and had youth training in the morning, and then was going to school for a double maths lesson in the afternoon. At sixteen he had been asked to train with the first team at his local Premier League club. He knew it was an impressive feat and he was excited for the prospect of new challenges and to show off at school. The day seemed to drag out ahead of him, his mind unfocussed on the schooling, it was a matter of years until he would never have to be in full time education again.

His brother, just sixteen months younger than him was following closely in his footsteps. He did not like to admit it, but he knew his brother would be better than him, with his brother managing to obtain all of the skills a year sooner than he had. He was pleased for his brother but jealous of his undeniable skill.

His brother was the clear favourite in the family and the jealousy, of course, stemmed from here, a deeply entrenched family dynamic which would set him into a try-hard sphere, spiralling off the track and ending up in a worse off position than when he had started, desperately yearning for his parents approval, their admiration, their praise.

He had been telling his brother about how all of the senior players were in training, which ones to look out for, which ones liked to try hard, and which ones pushed you over when the boss turned to nick the ball away, as well as coaching him about what to do when he received his own call up to the first squad.

He had said something stupid about his brother needing to try harder on the pass-backs in the box, being careful there was never a player looming just as he enjoyed doing. His comment was something he regretted now as his brother only looked up to him and would take on everything he said as positive criticism.

He made it through his mundane school day; this was the part which blurred out as he did not like to focus on arbitrary details. He survived until training and was ready and out on the field, kicking the ball about in a 3 v 2 and doing well if he thought so himself.

His forehead gleaming with delightful sweat, wiping it away with the back of his hand satisfyingly, admiring the way it shone in the sun. He was chatting away, socialising like a normal seventeen-year-old boy, cracking jokes and teasing other players.

It took one senior member of staff to change everything, the way he saw life, the way he interacted with others, he never spoke to his teammates in the same way, and it only took one person to pull him out of training early to do that.

Some solemn looking faces appeared at the side of the pitch whilst they had moved on to do some 5 v 5 drills and whispered to one of the coaches. He knew they were coming his way, all their eyes resting on his movements, on his actions, but he tried to act surprised when a hand placed itself on his shoulder and pulled him away from the ball and the other players.

They sat him down just outside of the clubhouse. The sweat was no longer satisfying to wipe off, steam pouring from his hair like a swirled hat, feeling faint and sick all at the same time. He was burning, boiling, sweltering under the blaring sun but as soon as the words left their lips, he felt cold, instantly.

This was the only part of the cassette tape which was damaged; their voices were distorted, as if they were speaking underwater. A garbled, warped sound which sounded like a language he had never heard of with only certain words standing out to him.

Your brother, accident, collapse, seizure, heart attack, hospital, life support.

He was rushed out of the training ground by someone he didn't know, a balding man with large sweat patches and a deep, cavernous voice trying to reassure him when he could not hear what he was saying, the feeling of a stranger taking him should have concerned him but all he did was sit in the car, staring out the window as the scenes blurred away, and allowed himself to be taken away from a painful place.

Little did he know at that time that the clubhouse was now a scarred place, tainted with blood and dirty memories. Every time he walked past the building, past the seat he had been forced to sit in, the water he had been forced to drink, he felt his stomach drop, his eyes hurt, his throat constricted.

He could hear it and see it all over again every time he would step out onto the field, and it was sunny.

But he was driven to the hospital closest to his house. His mother collected him from the door with a watery, half-hearted hug, rushing him through the doors where they found his dad pacing, his face pale and blotchy.

If he had thought the hours leading to football training had been slow, he could not believe how long the hours were which he spent in that hospital. Every minute felt like a day, waiting, and lifting their head at any doctor that walked past. Time was slower than it had ever been. Every sound was like an alarm, every footstep a warning sign. Each tick of the clock in the waiting room so agonising he wanted to tear it from the wall and hurl it across the room.

They sat and waited, his neck in pain from hanging so heavily, his head rested between his legs. He had not eaten since breakfast but the thought of food made him want to be sick.

His mind could not be distracted by anything else; he could not focus on anything other than the carpeted pattern on the floor of the waiting room. Counting the number of coloured circles imprinted into the beige carpet. Digging the studs of his boots into the brown.

Twenty-five, six, seven, eight-

Before it was too late.

There was nothing more they could do, they had tried everything and after looking at a scan of his brain they deemed if he were to wake, he would never be the same, he would be a shadow of himself, a lifeless human with no voice, no movement and no smile. If he woke.

And so, it was decided that all there was left to do was to turn off the life support machines and let him pass peacefully on, he should not be subject to a life without words, without emotion.

He had gone from chatting with his brother in the kitchen, kicking balloons in the direction of his dog, eating cornflakes with his brother, to seeing his eyes permanently shut, his face devoid of life and colour. Bags of fluids surrounding him filled with blood instead of fluid, his mouth blue, his tongue double the size, his ribs cracked, his body so small and timid. The last image he had of his brother. That was now the memory he had of his little brother. His brother was just fifteen years old.

That marked the day of his first memory of the voices in his head. They had started slow and infrequent, with the first voice reminiscent of his brothers. His voice was soft, calling out something every few days, sounding like an echo. He could hear him calling his name down the corridor at the football clubhouse, he heard his voice in a crowded room his calls desperate and needy, he could hear him laughing every time he tripped or caught his finger in a door.

It made him cry every time he heard it, how lifelike it was. How every time he believed his brother was around the corner.

And so, it soon changed and became a hollow, echoed voice, morphing away from his brother and eventually ruminated into the tone of his friend from home. It stopped making him cry. Not because the voice changed in tone, but because he became so numb to the sound of them. They became more of a comfort than a sorrow.

Slowly but surely the voices gained in confidence, they became more frequent and became louder. They found some friends and before he knew it, he was welcomed onto his eighteenth birthday by four persistent characters, singing and whistling in his ears.

Welcoming him to adulthood and letting him know he was not alone.

11. The Brutality of Football

He had tried hard, the almost six months he had been away, in his new life, not to think about that day. That day which still sent a hollow shiver down his spine, still shocked him to his core, still felt unbelievable when he really thought about it.

How could it have been prevented? Could he have noticed any signs? Were there any signs to notice?

His brother had never complained about anything in his life, never complained about being tired, being bored, being lonely.

He had never heard a negative word leave his brothers lips, he never would have come down one day and sat him down and said *listen Tom, I've been getting some weird fluttery yet pounding feelings in my chest, feels like my heart is trying to escape my body. It almost feels like my heart is failing.*

His brother never would have said that, and even if he had, would he have done anything. He would not have put it down to a myocarditis of his brother's heart; he would have called him unfit and told him to run laps around the garden. He would never have believed his fifteen-year-old brother had an actual malady which would soon actually fall out underneath him.

And now he was doing everything he never wanted to do, he was overthinking.

He was thinking about his brother, his last days on this earth, he was wondering if his brother was happy with his life. At that time, even he was happy with his life, he was happy with his family, happy with his football, happy with his social abilities and social media.

It all changed the day his brother died, and he became lost, he searched for his brother long and hard and even sometimes was convinced he could see him.

He never did.

Since that day he was a different person, he could not speak or joke with people, he could not feel happiness, he shut himself off completely and did the absolute bare minimum to survive.

And then all at once, without being informed that his time was up he found out that his period for grief was up. There was a cutoff point where everyone assumed the pain and the hurt just vanished and he could go back to being just as he was before. they assumed him to be the same person as if nothing had changed. It was expected that he could just act like a huge part of his body, his life, his soul had not just been torn away from him, and he was left with this gaping hole inside.

Everyone assumed the hole was all fixed up with the stipulation of time passing and that he could go on with life.

It was as if there had been a deadline he had not been told about where he was supposed to get over it all, he was never supposed to get sad about it, or God forbid let it affect his football.

He was talked about for months on television about how his game had been impacted by the sudden, tragic death of his brother but then the timer went, and they just criticised him, they said he was a short-lived success story and that he no longer possessed the magic touch they once thought he did.

It took him months more to get his reputation back, and to hide his brother's memory in a box until 90 minutes had been played so he was back in everyone's good graces.

It was almost unfathomable to anybody that he was still grieving. *Good God how is he not over the death, it was SIX months ago.*

It was six months following the death of his brother, his baby brother, and he was told he should be over it by now.

Is there ever a time limit for grief? Because it had been five years now and he still was not recovered. Not fully.

He remembered having to wait to be alone to get upset, to be sad, to have normal human feelings. But as these were not widely expected or accepted, they had to be constrained, they contorted inside of him at the sight of something that reminded him of his brother, they writhed around when someone mentioned his name, they punched him in the gut if he saw a picture of him or saw his mother crying again.

He waited to be alone to sob into his pillow. Sobbing so hard his body shook. His body ached and throbbed, convulsing without his consent and crying so desperately he felt like he was choking and drowning.

He lived with a permanent headache and bright puffy eyes for a month, every moment he was alone was a moment he spent thinking about him.

He never left his mind.

When seven months hit, he was taken back to the hospital. To the place he never wanted to return. The mundane face of the doctor telling his family there was no hope left. That the choice was in the hands of his parents, but their medical advice was to do nothing.

To end it all.

He remembered being tested for inflammation of his own heart. His body being scanned and pushed and probed and prodded until they confirmed he was safe; he would not die as suddenly as his brother had.

He did not know whether or not to feel relieved, part of him wanted to be reunited with his brother but that was selfish, wasn't it? His parents had already lost one son, could they bear to lose another?

He remembered sitting in hospital chairs and GP surgeries, waiting patiently alone. His parents made him the appointments but then failed to turn up to support him, deeming it was too painful and too difficult to be back in the hospital where they had lost their son.

They had not considered how it may have felt for him to be back there. Like the pain just missed him out because he never showed it.

His parents became empty shells in fact, they never quite recovered from the loss. They lacked emotion and empathy and yes, he knew that the pain they experienced losing a son was, is, unbearable; unthinkable, something you would never wish on your worst enemy. But their own grief thwarted the protection they needed to give their other son.

They failed to provide him with the support he desperately craved but could never form the words to ask for.

He never got to lie on his mother's lap while he wept about his loss and have her push his hair out of his eyes, smoothing it back in a motherly, comforting way. He never received that affection. And every day he would remind himself that it was because they had lost a son, a little boy, they had lost their child.

But whilst they had lost a child, they had each other, his parents had the same pain. They experienced the same loss. He had lost the only thing that made life worth living, not just his friend, not only his brother, but his soulmate for life. He had been taken away from him and it pained him that he could not remember the last words he spoke to him.

He no longer had a sibling, he had nobody else to grieve with, he was alone in his feeling as there were no sisters or brothers to share the pain with.

He was alone.

All he was left with now was the agony of the happy memories which he desperately wanted to relive, which he wanted to remember, but they caused him unimaginable grief.

The haunting sound of his little brothers laugh, combined with the ruinous fear that he would forget what the laugh sounded like or what his voice sounded like or what his brother looked like, and the terrible ache that he would probably have to wait decades to see him again.

Those feelings surged through him every day, every hour, every second. They followed him around both on and off the pitch. But for a few hours a day he had to ignore them and pretend they did not exist as that was the inevitable timeline, he had used up his grief period and now he had to move on, even if he still felt the same.

The timer had buzzed, people were waiting on him expectantly.

12. Ashes

It took them several weeks to decide just where his brother should be laid.

The ultimate resting place.

Several conversations were had over many days, over every meal, in every journey to and from training, some more heated than others.

They debated about where to scatter his ashes. Deciding what his brother had loved the most, deciding where his brother would have wanted to be. What his brother would want to be associated with.

It took a lot within him to hold back, to not spew all the horrible thoughts he had bubbling up in his body. They took over him and screamed at him.

The thoughts that he was the only one who genuinely knew his brother well. He had been the only one who had actually spent time with his brother by choice. Not by travelling to a football pitch, not because they were forced to due to eating a meal. They chose to spend their waking hours together. Every day they chose one another to speak to, to laugh with, to play games with.

The sensation gnawed at him, nibbling his insides away, the thought that he was the only one who knew what he truly loved.

But despite the hours on end, they spent side by side, the conversation of whether or not his fifteen-year-old brother would have wanted to be cremated and scattered across a football pitch or at the top of a mountain was as expected, left unsaid.

The cremation was no question, and whilst he knew that having the physical form of his brother's body was futile without the life within it, pressing the incineration button at the crematorium with his parents was one of the most onerous and haunting experiences he believed he would ever have to encounter.

Knowing that the simple act of forcing his finger against a button was removing the form his brother had held in his life. His brother's smile forever prevented from forming again, his brother's eyes permanently fused shut. His brother's body crumbled away, the body he would never be able to hug again.

That was painful and demanding.

But this, this was aggravating and taxing at this moment. He had not wished to be debating like this, just days, hours after his brother had been cremated.

The decision was made by his mother in the end. And her word was typically final.

He was to be split. His form divided across three locations.

One was in their home, in the garden, next to where they buried their rabbit who had been put down when he was ten, at the base of an old oak tree surrounded by wildflowers. This first location was insulting to him. He had loved the rabbit but to equate the burial of his brother to his rabbit was preposterous if not derogatory. He had not put up a fight at the time, and now he wished he had.

The second scattering took place at the pitches of course, at the place he fell. It had rattled him that they would want his ashes brothers to remain where his heart had stopped. Yes, his brother had loved football just as he had done, but his brother had never wanted it to be everything that defined him. And he found the sentiment resonated to his own life.

Finally, they took him to the park. A simple park that their parents had taken them both to during their childhood. Whilst they were growing up. Something so insignificant to him that he barely could grasp at the memory of the park in his head. The memory of it so faint it took him walking round it three times to remember just how they used to play. Taking in the old, rickety swing set, the rusted slide and fallen merry-go-round that no longer turned. It was dirty and overgrown, and he could see why they never went there anymore. But the park itself had meant so much to his mother, he could see her teary eyed as she described just where she wanted to scatter his brother that he could not possibly repudiate.

And so, he did not. And they spread his brother's ashes across three locations.

He got to walk past him every day when he walked onto the training ground pitches, passing the small garden they had scattered him across. Closing his eyes and wandering if he was really there when he quickened his pace so not to seem like he was loitering near his dead brother.

He never went to that patch in the garden, never walking to the end of the lawn to sit on the rotting bench next to the place where both his brother and his rabbit lay.

Once the ashes had been scattered at the park, he went back only one more time. Once when he was at his worst, at his most desperate. The time where he needed to speak to his brother the most. He could not speak to him at training, nor in the garden where his rabbit also lay, but also lay the prying eyes of his parents.

And so, he sat on an old swing, and he spoke to his brother. For the first time since the day. His words blended with tears.

Sobs.

They crumpled his body leaving him in a broken heap. Grappling at the swing set for comfort, for stability. Tears he had not shown outside of his room since the day and now he was afraid he would not be able to stop them.

To control them.

What hurt him the most was the grief he felt in not being able to say so many things. So many words left unsaid that he had not deemed important at the time. Words he had felt but did not want to appear weak or feeble for admitting aloud.

Plans had been made; hopes had been drawn out for both of them. Adventures and activities that were exclusive for the two of them, now implausible.

Once his apologies started to his brother they could not stop. Like the tears that kept on falling as did the list of his grievances. The sort of list that made him feel worse the deeper he delved into it.

It destroyed his own soul, the sadness he felt for himself that he was too cowardly to admit before, and the anguish that his brother would never get to hear them. Not properly.

He apologised for not trying harder to give him what he deserved.

For what he truly deserved was to be laid in water. Constantly moving and flowing. Invariably steady and everywhere. Not contained in the garden, or at the scene of the incident, not at a park his brother never would have remembered. He should have been one with the water, connected to everything, everywhere.

They should have taken his brother down to the seaside, to where he loved to visit on holiday. Taken his brother to his favourite spot by the ice-cream van and let him be free. Let his brother swim for the last time.

He knew this from the second they started deliberating where to take his brother. And he said nothing.

And for that, he would always be sorry.

13. Countdown

It was two days before his twenty-third birthday. Not that he was aware it was that soon. He thought he still had a week before he turned one year older.

His first celebration alone.

Not that he planned to celebrate.

He wondered if his parents were thinking of him, wondering if they considered how he was spending his birthday. It still pained him a little to think about them. If they were looking for him, if they were distraught with his absence.

He felt guilty, they had lost a child and he had left. Forcing them to lose two. But he could not go back just for them. He cared for them but he was finished in spending his life doing what they deemed appropriate.

For years he had done what they wanted, spent his hours doing what they desired.

It was time to do what he wanted, to carry out his dreams and wishes. He had done his best; he had been the best he had accomplished so very much. But it had not been right.

Maybe, had his brother still been alive it could have felt right. He and his brother could have played together on the same team, it sure was headed in that direction. But it could never be like that now.

And without his brother it did not feel right any longer. He did not love it like he used to.

14. Forced Grief

It came to the one-year anniversary. The first anniversary to mark his death. It rolled around far too quickly. Far too suddenly did it appear.

How had a year passed already?

It felt so inconceivably slow and yet somehow the fastest a year had passed. But all at the same time, it felt like no time had moved at all.

The incident may as well have been a day before, a week before. It still felt as fresh as that. It still felt so new and sharp and painful.

When it did come to the one-year mark he remembered it all. He remembered being given the day off, he remembered being told by his parents that it was alright to grieve, it was alright to take the day to be sad. He remembered the upmost pressure of being forced to grief on this particular day, as if the day was any more significant than the other three hundred and sixty-four that had passed already.

Why was the anniversary any different, any more painful than every other day?

Why was he given the special time to grieve?

He had felt particularly fine for that day, the shadow of grief was not as heavy on that day. And he remembered wanting to feel sad because it was expected of him. He forced the tears out so nobody would worry he had not taken this specially planned out day to be sad.

More than anything he was just confused.

Because every day was hard, not just the anniversary. Every day.

He had sworn himself to not cry anymore. These tears were fake. He had not cried for months, forcing himself to remain void of tears. He did not let them escape for any reason no matter how hard they stung at his eyes.

After his meltdown in the park, he had forbidden himself from crying again. Every whisper of sadness was buried deep within, forced down himself and shut away.

He wondered if anything would ever make him cry again.

He did not know what to do with himself on the day off. Playing football had become a good escape, a mindless task which he could focus on. It distracted him for a little while. But now he was left with nothing to do. No football, he had not attended school in a year, he had nothing.

His parents had taken the car and driven off, taking themselves on a tour of the country to take their mind off the day.

But they had left him behind. Another forgotten thought as he turned out to be.

But he was not as forgotten as he believed. One person was still there, one person still showed up outside of his house after training.

His friend.

Carrying a takeaway pizza under one arm, smiling already as he opened the door, his friend invited himself in. He never addressed the day, nor the forced sadness he was supposed to feel. But his friend knew.

He knew all too well.

His friend chattered mindlessly throughout the night, not allowing a moments silence to rest between them. He had believed at the time that it was to distract him from thoughts he was supposed to have of his brother. But on reflection, it seemed more likely that his friend was doing it to prevent his own thoughts. His friend had too seen him like a brother, and he too had lost someone.

And in the darkness of his self-loathing grief, where he spiralled into a lonely slump, envisaging himself as the only mourner who felt his pain, he had forgotten about his friend. His friend who had always been with them, who had been next to him on the sofa when they played videogames, who had been walking beside them on the way to the park, who had driven them home from training.

He may not have truly had another sibling to share in the grief, but with someone like his friend, he felt the pain was lifted.

15. A Friendly Face

Once six months in his new home rolled around, almost like clockwork on the morning of the sixth month (not that he knew it was six months yet), he felt a certain longing for the past. He was desperate to see what life was like without him.

Feeling self-centred he wondered if people were still talking about his disappearance, he was not even aware if they had ever spoken of his disappearing act. He was interested to see if anything had changed in the time he had been away. Half a year had passed, something must have changed, even if that something was him.

But most importantly, he was running out of food. He had packed what he believed to be years' worth of food in his car before he left, unperishable items he knew he would not enjoy but could live off and never have to leave.

Now here he was, standing in front of empty cupboard shelves, with only a single pack of instant noodles in front of him, that would make it his fourth packet this week. His stomach grumbled and churned, he felt sick at the idea and his body refused it. He wanted fresh food, he wanted vegetables and fruits and juices and bread and a warm home cooked meal.

His stomach garbled again, he wanted the juiciness of a thick, rubbery mushroom, tearing into the soft delicate roll which melted in his mouth, he wanted the warm sensation of melted cheese.

Cheese, he knew what he wanted, and he knew exactly where to go to get it.

He knew there had been closer places to visit that would have provided him with the fix of food he desired. But he could not help the alluring temptation of coming back home, just for a couple of hours. He wanted to see if life had stayed just the same, he knew he was kidding himself thinking that everything would be different just because he had vanished. And yet he was still slightly disappointed that everything was the exact same as when he left it a few months ago.

This was his first visit back to civilisation, his first experience back surrounded by people. It felt busy the second he stepped out of his car; his breath felt stifled as if he was choking on air. Dirty air that had been breathed in and out by thousands of different lungs, it was not pure like the air around his home, it felt like he was inhaling the air from the smoking area of a club, cigarettes, and marijuana filling his lungs and occluding his airways.

The second he started to walk away from his car he regretted going there. His body froze and he stood planted on the spot, watching people rush past, mothers and babies, school children in their uniforms, groups of boys sitting on walls and smoking.

The air was humid and damp, the floor had sheen from rain on it and he felt hot under his clothes, his back already starting to collect sweat. His hands began to tremble, his palms too turned to sweat, that choking, gagging shortness of breath he thought he was imagining was real and sat in his throat blocking his trachea and impairing his breath.

His fingers fumbled with his clothes, his chest feeling painful and sharp. He did not know what to do or how to react this was unbearable.

He almost turned back but the pains in his stomach whined away and begged him to keep going. He needed food and then he would disappear again, hopefully for another six months or longer.

He walked past a place he knew far too well; it was the local café him and his brother used to visit every afternoon after football training while they waited to be picked up by a parent. It smelt of cinnamon and coffee and he found himself pressed up against the window, drooling and tearing all at the same time.

His emotions were all over the place, he knew he looked almost homeless, with hair now down past his shoulders almost reaching his nipples, his clothes which he had forced on himself were baggy and he looked generally unkempt.

He was a mess of a person, but he hoped that meant people would avoid looking at him for too long, and as a result would not recognise him. He pushed open the door to the café and sat down in the usual seat he recognised, except the chair opposite was empty. This was the first time he had felt the courage to re-enter something so close to him, something he knew would trigger his memories.

Deep breaths, and eyes shut he managed to hold back tears. He was handed a menu, and someone muttered something incoherently, or it may have been audible, but he could not hear it, he did not want to hear it. He took the menu and scanned it, passing it immediately back and ordering a three-cheese omelette and a hot chocolate.

He had tried to be a vegan since leaving six months ago but the temptation and the desire for cheese was agonising, the want for milk chocolate made him drool. The lady who handed him the menu scuttled off after he followed his desires, dragging her feet, and walking with a slight wobble to her. He sat back in the chair and took another deep breath.

He allowed himself to scan the room, he allowed himself to remember.

His brother used to always get the omelette, if he was being honest, he hated eggs but today it just felt right to order it. Usually, he would get something boring like porridge and tell his brother that if he wanted to be called up to the first team, he would have to start weighing his food and counting his calories, his protein, and his natural fat.

He regretted telling him off about something so trivial now like eating chocolate and cheese and wished he had just too ordered a three-cheese omelette and indulged in a slice of triple layered chocolate cake after to share. It was all too easy to regret when someone isn't around anymore, when there is nothing, you can do to change it or rectify the situation.

You could sit and regret the day away, you could lay and remember all the memories you have and debilitate yourself with the feeling that you will never make a new memory with them, or you will never get to invite them to occasion that are so important to you that you know they would appreciate.

His brother would have loved his new home, he would have invited him out there. He would have given him a key and let him stay whenever he wanted, but he would never see it, he would never know about it, and he would never come and stay with him in the cabin in the woods.

He realised he was sending himself into a downwards spiral and he did not want to start the reminiscent tears here in the centre of the café, so he distracted himself once again with the other members in the room. They were side characters in the story about himself and so their role was vital in shaping his experience here today.

There was the mother and daughter talking in loud, aggressive tones, the daughter was wearing tights with holes in them and short shorts that allowed him to have an open view of her bottom, he turned away to allow her some decency.

He looked over at the old man sat in the corner alone, he wondered if that is what he would be like in years to come. But he was soon distracted by the little boy throwing peas at his older sister who was screaming at him to stop. And then there was the lady who-

A three-cheese omelette was placed in front of him, alongside a steaming hot-chocolate; the cream was already melting away into the liquid. He smiled up gratefully, the lady with the wobbly walk smiled back but it turned quickly to a frown as it looked like she tried to focus on his face. He turned away quickly and focussed on the food. Shovelling it into his mouth so quickly he scorched his tongue. He did not even remember what it tasted like, or if he even liked it but it was disappearing down himself. Before he knew it the plate was empty, the residue of cheese oil dripped across his plate, and he rested his cutlery down neatly in the centre.

He sat back and almost like clockwork the voices chirped up in his head, he hadn't heard them for a few days, and it felt nice to be fully alone for once. But they came back in full force, with a series of voices he did not recognise.

He had never heard the child's voice before, or that girl, or an elderly man. And then he realised that the voices were not in his head, but outside of his head and they were around him. They were yelling out at him in the café.

It was all too much. He could hear the people whispering about him as if they were standing right next to him, practically screaming about him into his ear. Their voices sounded hushed, but it was not hard to hear them, to make out what they were saying. Well, it was all too obvious that they were trying to be heard by him. He was sat in the centre of the café, his head down, his hands running through his hair trying to cover his face. They were all watching him, they were pointing and whispering behind their hands, and he could hear them. He could "HEAR" them.

He ran outside and fell to the floor, slumped against a wall. But he could not catch his breath; the voices were still ringing in his ears he could still hear them whisper his name in harsh tones, they had nothing nice to say about him. He covered his ears and rocked back and forth; his eyes squeezed as tightly shut as he could get them.

His head felt heavy, his chest pounding. Why had he come back?

He should have known people would stare and point and laugh. They had spoken about him as if he had not been in the room.

His body shook with each rock on his ankles, trembling, quivering. Sweat was pouring from every orifice, collecting in that place it loved to go down his underwear.

'Tommy?'

He opened one eye, and all at once it was silent. The voices vanished, ran away from him when they saw he had brought in back up.

He had come in with protection.

He looked up blankly. Still sat, knees pulled into his chest on the floor. His hair was a knotted mess, and his eyes were bright red and streaming.

'Oh my God, Tommy.' His friend's face dropped, the expression on his face was relief, anger, elation and upset all at the same time.

He eventually scrambled himself up and pulled his hair out of his face, quickly wrapping it into a knot which moderately replicated a bun behind his head. Wiping his eyes he nodded once at his friend, acknowledging him but displaying no emotion, not saying a word. Almost terrified that he was standing before him.

His friend hugged him tight; he stayed stiff, not moving his arms from his side. Unsure of how to feel, how to act. He wanted to run, but he could not bear to leave his friend again.

His friend pulled away, mouth open, then closed, then open again. His friend was stunned to silence.

'What are you doing here, Tommy?' his friend finally spoke. It had not meant to, but his friend's words came across more accusatory than intended. He was a little surprised by the tone.

He shrugged it off, chuckled and stepped back away from his friend, backing against the wall of the cafe.

'Nice to see you too.' He matched the bitterness in tone.

'Don't you worry, I'm leaving now,' he said bluntly, turning away forcefully.

His friend grabbed his arm, and he froze, letting the warmth of his friend's hand wrap its way around his wrist.

'No, I'm not saying leave, Tommy. I meant, after all of this time, why are you here?' His friend threw his arms to the side, bewildered, his face the vision you'd imagine had you just seen a ghost.

He watched his friend's face for a moment. His friend was fortunate in having wonderfully admirable features; curly hair, which he knew was the bane of his friend's existence because of the self-care routine he was burdened with. His friend had dark, olive like skin, with green tinged brown eyes, deep set in his face with a strong nose and thick lips all perfectly proportioned. He also knew his friend had brilliantly white, straight teeth but he couldn't see them now, neither boy was smiling at the other.

'I just came today to get something to eat,' he spoke simply, the corners of his mouth twitching up. He knew he was being terribly irritating and yet he could not disclose anything else. He could not risk proclaiming his situation or his purpose.

He cared about his friend more than he liked or wished to admit, but he had been missing for six months and there had been little effort from anybody to find him. At least that was what he believed was the case. The voices in his head had driven him down a spiralised hole where he finally concluded that nobody missed him, and why would you go searching for someone you didn't miss.

His friend looked visibly frustrated; he smiled a little.

'Okay, come on then,' his friend said, with little delay.

His friend put one of his hands on his back, gesturing for him to walk alongside.

He looked back in confusion.

'Where?'

His friend let out a dry, lifeless laugh.

'You just said you came to get something to eat. Let's go eat. We can go and get some ice-cream or something. You look like you need to eat.'

His friend applied more pressure to his back, gently forcing him to take a step.

'I cannot get ice-cream,' he said plainly, watching the expression on his friend's face alter and skew.

His friend stopped, letting his arm rest on his back. He smiled internally at the pressure and the warmth of another human touching him.

'Why not?' his friend asked innocently, expecting some great response, some plan to why the boy standing before him had skipped town without a word and now had mysteriously reappeared.

Where could he need to go at a time like this? What did he do with his days? Where did he live? What did he eat? Will he ever come back?

'I'm a vegan now,' he slipped out, knowing fully well he had just devoured not moments ago a three-cheese omelette and deeply rich and bitter hot chocolate with whole milk, gelatine marshmallows and full-fat cream on top.

His friend let out a heartier laugh, it wasn't full, but it sounded like it had more spirit in it, shaking his head in disbelief.

'Okay. Let's go get some fucking vegan ice-cream then,' his friend mused forcing him alongside.

They walked side by side, neither speaking just letting the silence fill the space between them. He felt tired just keeping up with his friend's long strides and realised he had ignored the fact he had lost weight. He had lost both muscle and fat and was now weaker than ever before. He resembled the strength of a six-year-old boy, not an alleged twenty-three-year-old man.

It made sense why he lost weight, as he often forgot to eat. At football training beforehand they would make you eat, set breakfasts, set lunches, and then he would go home, and his mum would have cooked for him, something off the set menu he had been sent home with by his dietician. He was always fed what he was supposed to, he had never had to worry about eating before, he had a plate put in front of him and he ate, never to enjoy just filling a hole and because he knew he had to.

Now that he was in charge, he found he just…forgot. He regularly skipped meals and often would go the whole day without eating anything and not even realising, his body was no longer hungry for food. It was hungry for satisfaction; his satiety came in the form of feeling accomplished. He was too preoccupied by other things, more exciting things.

It felt uncomfortable from the start, when his friend saw him, when they walked together, when they sat down across the table from each other in cold, rickety chairs. There was a palpable tension in the air, he did not notice it of course but his friend did.

His friend felt the time that had passed between them, not recognising the man sitting in front of him now. He had changed a little since they had last seen each other. His hair was longer of course, sitting past his clavicles, his eyes were hollowed and darker, they had aged and tired since he had left. His face was skinner, and bonier but he still had the same characteristic smile, the same laugh, the same tone of voice. Except everything he said had lost all feeling, lost all meaning and was monotone, he had been stripped of emotion.

His friend barely knew what to say, after all what do you say first to someone who ran away from the life of fame and fortune, his family, and friends, to be a recluse in a lost cabin.

'So, what have you been doing?' His friend, after frantically scanning his brain for something suitable to say, finally landed on a question that seemed appropriate.

It was definitely not the first thing on his friend's mind, but he believed starting with a gentle question could lead to probing after.

He shrugged at first, pursing his lips and refusing to give anything away. He drew his fingers across the table, using the left-over liquid that the last people had left to draw out his name in swirly clear fluid.

His friend sighed. 'Tommy,' his friend said softly, drawing his eyes up from the table. And it was as if the sound of his name on his friends lips had loosened his own lips and tongue, he sat up and the words just slipped out from his mouth uncontrollably. Word vomit.

'Everything really, I like to paint, I read, I cook, I write, I walk, I swim, I run.' His tone increased in pace as he excited himself with his list. 'I do everything, and anything I want to.' He now could not help himself from smiling at his own achievements. 'I live alone in the woods, in a wooden cabin, and nobody ever comes near me.'

His chest felt heavy as he recited off everything, things he was finally proud of, everything he actually enjoyed doing. His friend smiled too, it was a weaker smile, it barely matched his own, but it was there. It may have been forced but he could tell that his friend only wanted what was best for him.

'Why?' Was all his friend could ask, barely able to get the word out.

'Because I wanted to.' He said as if it were the most obvious reason. 'It is my life.'

'That is no life, Tommy.' His friend probed.

'Sure it is, I wanted it, I created it, it is my life.' His friend shook his head with every word he said.

'This is the first time you have ever been able to choose something yourself, just because you chose it does not make it right. It does not make it a life, Tommy.'

He frowned.

It was his life. He had made a home, a routine. He had lasted six months perfectly fine.

'And what about your job, your career, what about football?' His friend continued to challenge him.

'I have made a choice to not touch a football ever again.'

He dictated clearly. 'Doubt I'd be any good at that thing now,' he added, scoffing slightly.

His friend's smile faded quickly, he frowned and sat back in his chair.

'That thing is my passion,' his friend said, slightly bitterly. 'And I believed it was your passion as well. You were a star, and idol, you had the most skilful game play I think I have ever seen. You were…are so gifted. And yet, you did not want any of it.' His friend almost sounded resentful; his tone acetous. 'We needed you on our team, and you just left us. Without a word!'

He was shocked; he did not expect him to be so accusatory about his choices. It seemed like nobody had cared about him when he was around, and it was now only when he had vanished, that they realised just how desperately he was required.

'Maybe the team should have expressed their desire for me before,' he said superficially, his crudeness cutting through his friend turning his head away.

'I always did,' his friend responded curtly, his tone was forceful and firm. 'I always showed you the respect and admiration that you deserved.'

He looked back at his friend, whose face was softer and kinder. He looked remorseful and penitent. He almost felt sorry for him. Their ice-creams were brought over to the table, and they had to stifle any thoughts that had entered their minds. They politely smiled at the waitress who handed them their respective orders, the sort of polite smile where you purse your lips and turn the corners of your mouth out and nod at the same time. They both did it in turn and waited until she was out of sight before they dared to look at one another again. His friend then waited until he was comfortable, waited until he was mid-lick through an ice-cream, waited until his legs were crossed, his eyes were closed, and he was backed into a situation he could not escape.

'So, when are you going to tell me what is actually going on?' his friend said, letting his own ice-cream rest on the table, untouched.

He sat back and sighed, shaking his head, his eyes fluttering shut, his friend leaned forward impatiently.

'People thought you had died, Tommy. This is serious.'

His friend's voice turned harsh, his words like little swords cutting through the air.

He shook his head, shrugging.

'But I'm fine,' he spoke nonchalantly, brushing his friend aside with one hand gesture, averting his gaze back down to his name across the table. The droplets of water had coagulated and congealed in the centre of the shiny metal surface again.

His friend seethed across the table, watching him sit back, relaxed as ever, but his friend's hands clasped tight onto the chair as if to hold himself back.

'I can see you're fine, what I want to know is why you left without a word.'

He hesitated, watching his friend clench and unclench his jaw periodically.

He shook his head. 'I left for the greater good, I left for everyone's benefit. I left for you, for the team, for my parents, but mostly I left for myself,' he spoke as if he was reading off a poem. The nuances of his words rising and falling with a natural breath.

His friend frowned but his face was relaxed.

'It wasn't the life for me,' he said honestly. 'I couldn't do it anymore; I wasn't being me. I had to get away to find where I should be.'

He tried to search for empathy in his friend's facial expressions but struggled to find it. He thought of all people, that his friend would understand at a time like this. In the past he had understood everything before.

'And what about when you kissed me? Were you being you then?' his friend asked.

He froze, stunned to speak.

He had completely forgotten about the kiss, either that or it had been forced to the back of his mind by the voices in his head. They locked it away in a deep, dark cavern where only they could find it, password protected with some dragon guarding the entrance. The voices in his head were protecting him from his own memory by keeping it away from him. He wasn't sure how to react and so he didn't he just sat still and left his face unmoved, undetected, emotionless hoping that if he just stayed silent the problem would fade away.

It didn't.

'Tommy, you kissed me,' his friend continued, his voice cracking as he spoke. 'And then disappeared the next day and I didn't hear from you for six months.'

His friend now had the start of tears in his eyes, which he did not understand. Why was he so upset?

'I came to your house the morning after, I don't know why, I was going to make something up about driving you to training but I was coming to see you. And your mum told me you were not in your room and your car was not in the drive so you must have already gone. I worried at that point about what you were doing, going to training over an hour early, but really, I should have been concerned about you running off to a creepy old cabin in a remote wood where nobody could possibly find you.' His friend paused, looking for some form of validation or recognition in his face. He gave his friend nothing. 'And then you get upset nobody is looking for you? What is going on, Tommy?' His friend was upset. It was only for a second, but tears flashed in his eyes, one looked like it was ready to fall, his friend blinked them away.

He sat motionless; he knew it was his turn to speak but he was unsure of what next to say.

'I'm sorry,' felt like the right thing to say. His words still contained little emotion, a forced apology.

His friend scoffed and turned away momentarily, but his bout of anger was yet to pass.

'Do you understand how many people have been missing you and care about you and have been worried about you?'

His friend was frantic, his voice raising higher, and higher, faster, and faster. He looked vacant, his eyes hollow and bleak.

'Nobody will care to notice; nobody will care to look. Nobody misses you.' He repeated the words the voices in his head had spoken; word for word he recounted what they had said. He was dead behind his eyes.

His friend sat back, raising his arms to his side, and then dropped them down again. His mouth opened and closed several times before he spoke again.

'Clearly, you don't understand because you wouldn't have done this if you've known you'd known.'

He sighed again and put his ice cream down for the first time, grief crossing his brow for a second.

'I'm sad you don't seem to understand.' He shook his head. 'I really thought you would, you of all people.'

His friend reacted by freezing and sat still, he wasn't sure how to react or what to say. His friend studied him carefully, his thin neck and pale, almost translucent skin stretched over his narrow cheeks and forehead. He looked sickly.

'Then why could I not have known?' His friend was challenging him now. Playing with his emotions.

'You would have told me to stay.' He said firmly.

'Yes,' his friend nodded, 'I would have.'

'I could not stay.' He was stubborn.

He was changed. He was determined to keep up his new life. He wished to be alone in his cabin once again. Something he would not have known had he not come to the town today. It was obvious he was not meant to be around others. At the sight of their pointing, or at the end of their whispers. He was meant to be locked away, with just some water and the sun as his only accomplices.

'I think you should come back home, Tommy,' his friend finally announced.

He instantly shook his head, a smile crawling across his cheeks.

He laughed.

'I am not leaving.' Each word was dictated carefully, giving a dramatic pause between the syllables.

His friend's face grew with impatience again, his eyes narrowed, they were a little terrifying.

'Tommy, there is a lot going on that you are not aware of. Things that require you.' His friend hesitated. 'Your parents need you; they miss you; they are terrified—'

'These are things they could have addressed with me before; it is too late now.' He dismissed every comment with a swipe of his hand.

'Tommy, I think you should know that your grandad is unwell,' his friend said, softening his tone briefly. 'You need to come back to see him, he too is asking after you.' His friend felt almost silly trying to convince him. He felt a shiver of guilt, a wave of anguish but brushed it off. He knew there was no way his granddad would ever ask after him, he was the child nobody cared about, why would he be sought after? Surely, he was asking for his brother, well they could be reunited soon. The self-pity nibbled away at his skin.

His face was detached from the whole conversation, he could barely make any eye contact.

'Well, everyone has to die eventually,' he said after a pause.

His friend drew out a ragged breath, it hitched when he realised that he was no longer who he thought he was.

'Tommy, what is going on, this isn't like you at all.' His friend tried to reason with him. The voices in his head started screaming, screaming so loud it hurt his ears and gave him a headache.

They were shouting at him to get out of the situation, get away from this human who clearly didn't know him like they did. They told him they're protecting him, and the best form of protection is to get up from the table, no flip the table out of anger, and walk off, stalk off, and get back in your car and drive away. And never come back here ever again, never speak to this boy, never think about him. This boy doesn't know him or respect his decisions.

'No. This is exactly like me,' he finally said, his friend covered his face with his hands. 'This is who I am now.'

16. The Mistake

Time felt endless, it dragged out, each minute lasting an hour, each hour lasting what felt like days. The weather became darker, cloudier, and muggier and more humid. The two boys were caught at a crossfire staring each other down. Who would be the first to break? Who would crumble under the intense gaze of the other? He noticed small things about his friend that had changed, his friend lived for the butterfly mantra, but the necklace he was used to seeing hanging from his friend's neck was missing. The neck now looking bare and empty without its usual pendant swinging against it. He continued to drum his fingers against the silver metal table in front of him, making the passing seconds even more awkward with his need to be constantly moving or doing something.

In truth this is not how he had envisaged seeing his friend again, he had hoped it would be quite the opposite, an open armed hug and a tear of happiness shed, not out of anger. He had thought about it a lot.

On some days, in the past, when he was thinking about his friend, his mind would get ahead of itself. It was so busy most of the time that it could often run off in several directions and he had to choose which to follow. Would it be the sinister, bad news breaking voice leading him down a treacherous path lined with black hanging trees shading the way down a black hole? Would it be the bright illuminated face walking along a path made of clouds and giggling away to itself, that voice was particularly alluring.

Or one of the other three, the monotone, depressed, lonely voice, whose path was raining and sodden, the youthful, innocent, and hopeful voice who would skip down a yellow brick road off into the sunset.

He could never decide which path was best to follow but he had seen them so many times, he had observed the same scenario countless times that he had almost visited them all.

It was the hopeful voice he followed on the day where he found himself kissing his best friend. He found it slightly invigorating and sent tingles around his body at the prospect. The voice singing in his ear as he felt the soft, powdery lips of his friend. Of course, he had no idea what they actually felt like, but the voice made it seem oh so very exciting, delicious and perfect.

He had replayed that scenario many times, choosing that one more than he would care to admit. He would follow the young child, skipping alongside them, sometimes hand in hand, sometimes he was chasing behind them, and sometimes, when he knew the scenario well, he was running ahead of the child. The yellow pathway would soon fade into a bedroom, that bedroom he could draw out he knew it so clearly. The cream to white walls, the low bed with grey pillows and throw, the fuzzy rug under his feet, the Aztec curtains. He had been to his friend's room just a few times in real life, but thousands of times in his mind.

It did not matter what the room looked like, what mattered is that he was sat on the bed with his friend, talking and laughing and smiling like they always did. And before he knew it, they were kissing, and he liked it. He felt a warm, comfort from being close to his friend, and he liked the way he could almost sense his friend's skin despite him not being in the room.

Sometimes he thought to himself, not in a dream state, but in reality, about kissing his friend for real to see if it was like he imagined, but also because he was so very desperate to do so.

It had been the day before he left. He knew in his mind he was leaving the next morning, he had planned it to perfection. Every detail sought out and completed. And he could not well say goodbye to his friend because that would have been too obvious, but he also could not hide the feelings he had developed for his friend and the enticement he felt about kissing him.

What was worse was that he knew the feelings were growing and yet they still felt like they had creeped up on him.

He had started to catch himself staring, smiling, and thinking about his friend more than he should have been. Always trying to find his friend in a room, seeking out his gaze and allowing his cheeks to fill with colour when his friend smiled at him.

He would have to distract himself in the day to stop his mind wandering about where his friend may be, or what he was doing, or if he was thinking about him too.

It was not until he was in bed, at night, with the lights off and the covers over himself, and he was sure he would be undisturbed, that he would allow himself to think, to dream, to explore what it would be like to be with his friend. In his room all alone, he could imagine whatever he wanted, he could imagine himself touching his friend, and feeling his curly hair, and finding out what his lips felt like. It was in those moments where he found his feelings ran away from him, and he knew it was too late. He knew there was nothing he could do about it; he knew there was no way he would be able to ever act on these emotions that had formed within him.

He also had determined that it was not something fleeting, as once the feeling arrived, it stayed, for a year at least, ever prominent, and ever powerful; a throbbing, intense, passionate desire to know what it was like to be close to someone else.

He waited, very patiently, until they were alone, until they were together sat next to each other, knees brushing accidentally, deep in conversation, he was always listening, his friend always chattering, but he laughed at everything his friend said. They had been sat just outside of the training ground, sharing a "cheat" Oreo milkshake from a stand down the road.

Taking slurps from the cardboard cup each before passing it over and talking about something funny that someone had done at training that day. He waited until that moment when the laughter died down and they caught each other's eye and decided it was now or never. An insurgence of confidence and exhilaration drove him forwards. He kissed his friend, it was quick and light, but he still kissed his friend. His friend did not push him away, but he did not kiss him back. His friend had sat, unmoved like a plank of wood, holding onto the paper cup, frozen in time, like he had just kissed a tree, with no passion or desire like he had imagined. And when he pulled away, he said nothing, his friend said nothing, they stared at each other for a minute.

Silence resumed.

And so, he got up and left. He said nothing to his friend, and he allowed his friend no time to say anything to him. And then he left for good the next day.

It had not been the kiss he had imagined so many times before. And it had been that second, he decided his friend was never to be seen again.

Now six months later, his friend stumbled across him and found him crumpled in a heap on the street, gripping to the wall of a café like his life depended on it. His friend had come to take him back, or at least try to.

Though he knew what he should do, the voices in his head were telling him what to do.

He could not.

He could not take his eyes off his friend, the same feeling he had fought hard to ignore for six months had resurged. His stomach fluttering, twisting and turning with every flutter of an eyelid, every turn of a lip, every hint of a smile.

Every single emotion rushed through him, and he could no longer be enraged.

He defied the voices in his head. He did not flip the table over and leave defiantly.

Instead, he decided to invite his friend to see where he lived. Maybe then he could understand why he decided to leave, maybe then he would see his side of things and he would encourage him to stay. Instead of being dragged back to his shiny, untouched home with his cold parents and empty lifeless bedroom.

No, he instead would show his friend the cabin; he was showing off his brand-new home. He had obtained a promise from his friend that the location and contents of the cabin were a complete secret, and he could never tell a single sole where he was living.

His friend had been unsure, he had tried to argue for him to stay. But reluctantly, his friend had agreed, too believing that their time together did not need to be over just yet.

17. Time to Talk

They had driven in silence, his friend had climbed into his car with great reluctance, making sure to note every small detail in the car. His friend's eyes would dart around the vehicle, out the front window, behind him on the seats, down onto the floor, always resting his final gaze on him. He knew his friend was attempting to identify anything he could decipher about his life. He tried to ignore the blatant panic in his friend's eye and instead smiled every time he felt he was being watched. He did not know the route well but took it slow, he knew he would be led there by instinct.

It took him almost double the time to reach back to the fortress of trees than it had to leave. When he eventually turned the hum of the engine off, they both sat, staring out in front of them. His friend was clasping the seat.

'Are we here?' his friend asked, glancing out the side window briefly. The darkness had set, its grey haze settling around them and obscuring their view.

He nodded and slowly lifted himself out the car, rushing around the front to open the door for his friend. His friend got out quickly and stood behind him. The air was still and warm but wet at the same time.

'This way,' he grumbled, leading the way between the trees to his lost cabin. He opened the door and let himself in, holding it for his friend to follow him through. 'I know it may seem like not much, but I don't need much.' He found himself justifying the small holes in the wood, the musty smell, the darkness of the whole room merely lit by two dingy lamps.

The room felt cold, colder than outside and he was immediately conscious that his friend may feel it too.

His friend said nothing as he made his way around the cabin, looking at the unmade bed, the piles of books and drawings, the paint he now wished he had sorted out, the pan from last night's instant noodles he had not washed up. He felt conscious and he felt his back sweating a little.

'This is where you have been living?' his friend finally asked, his voice small and timid. He continued to observe his friends eyes scanning the room.

He nodded. His friend looked away again, taking in the room for another time.

'I like it,' his friend said, his voice even smaller than before.

His friend's gaze was now approving, smiling, admiring. Relaxation spread down him as he watched his friend now reach out and touch objects within his home. His friend glinted at the puzzles, brushed against the stacks of books, fingered between the pages of drawings and paintings.

He kept his eyes fixed on his friend, trailing his steps across the room until he dragged himself over to the bed and sat on it carefully. He continued to watch as his friend traipsed around, making mental notes of everything. Eventually, after what must have been ten minutes his friend was satisfied with the mental images he had made of this lost cabin.

He waited for his friend to sit down on the chair across from the bed, the chair at the desk, which was dark oak, scattered with pages of crinkled artwork. His friend held up a quick sketch he had made of the lake, his friend pointed at the landscape and commented on the detail and how lifelike it was. He smiled bashfully; his cheeks reddened.

Flicking through the work he had cultivated over the last few months. Paintings of the lake, of the trees, sketches of animals, or insects. A final drawing, he had done from memory. A drawing of his friend.

His friend pulled out that picture and studied it intently. Holding it close to his face and then at an arm's length.

'I think it looks like me.' He smiled, returning the drawing to the stack on the chair.

It was only when his friend had moved away that he realised he had been holding his breath. Hoping for his friends approval.

Instead of sitting across from him, his friend took a seat on the bed next to him. A position they had been in many times before but now set him on edge. His body recoiling as far away as it could.

They were once again staring at each other, wondering what to say. His friend went first and said the one thing he had always been thinking but had been too afraid to say.

'Your brother would have loved it here,' his friend sighed as he spoke.

His friend had been the one person after him who had known his brother to the core, the sort of knowing that was so deep you could picture his thoughts and feelings, his words and phrases, the sounds he would have made. He tensed up at the mention of his brother but nodded in agreement.

Silence resumed.

'You know your parents do miss you.' His friend was reluctant to speak this time.

Just like his friend knew his brother, he also knew him, and knew about the relationship he had cultivated with his parents since the death.

'They want you back,' his friend pressed. He looked up, the light had vanished from his eyes and black holes resumed.

The colour had drained from his face and any emotion that had peeked its head out was now absent, a blank face with dull eyes and no smile. He took the silence to shake his head timidly, such small movements they may not have even been present. His friend persisted.

'I know it has been hard.' His friend's voice was trailing away, losing confidence with every movement, every sound, every syllable. 'I cannot begin to imagine how you must feel, but…'

He looked up expectantly, but his eyes were more ferocious than he realised, his friend halted, waiting for an outburst. Nothing came.

'They're still your parents, and they miss you, and love you, and if you're doing this to torture them then I think your point has been made,' his friend carried on. 'They've lost one son already, don't make them lose another.'

It was at this moment he decided to scoff; it was soft but still very apparent. His friend pursed his lips in return.

'They've had five years,' he finally spoke; he wasn't sure what he was going to say. He feared for himself, for his friend, it had been so very long since he had broken down, since he had an outburst; the constricting, burning, choking feeling was swirling around inside him.

The burst was coming, he could no longer suppress his emotions, but he didn't want to explode now, leaving splatter across the room, across his friend. He wanted to keep it bottled up, the pain of the pressure constricting his lungs, preventing him from breathing. He held his breath, hoping to force the feeling down, his chest tightened, it burned, it was a fiery pit and it was scorching his skin, it was burning a hole through his skin, singing his muscles and gnawing through his ribcage.

'Five years.' The words dribbled down his chin. 'To tell me how they felt, to make me feel like…' He let out a small scream, the pain was excruciating, there was no stopping it. He couldn't control it any longer.

'To make me feel like I was their son!' he screamed.

His head tilted up to the ceiling, his arms clutching at his sides, hoping to keep himself together.

'Tommy,' his friend was almost begging.

'They made me feel like a stranger, like someone who knew their son but not very well, someone who would pass by and was shocked by it but not impacted.'

It felt like venom passing through his lips, charring his teeth, and searing his lips as they left them, poisoning him. He felt tears coming, his eyes blistering by the pain behind them.

'My brother…'

He felt his throat closing in on him. He couldn't even say the word died. He felt ridiculous, his arms at his side limply as he stood there like a mute.

Your brother died, GET OVER IT.

That was a harsh one from one of the voices.

'Tommy,' his friend called to him. 'It is okay to be sad, it is okay to still be grieving,' his friend continued; he closed his eyes tightly. 'Tommy, just tell me, tell me everything you feel and regret. Get it all out in the open.'

He shook his head, his eyes were on fire, begging for a tear outlet but he wouldn't let them fall. He kept blinking back his tears, not wanting to cry about it in front of his friend, he was yet to cry about it in front of anyone.

His friend spoke softly. 'Tommy,' he said knowingly. 'You know you can tell me anything.' His friend's voice was smooth, like soft butter running against toast, gliding across his skin.

His sucked in through his teeth.

'I can't,' he eventually said, feeling heavier by the second. 'There's nothing to say,' he said firmly, his chest was shattered; he knew the outburst was far from over but he had to try and contain himself.

His friend sat back in his chair, watching his face carefully. He didn't look up but rested his eyes on his friend's shoes. He watched them shuffle, they jolted up and down, his friend was either impatient or had some kind of mobility tick he had never noticed before. Now he couldn't tear his eyes away, counting the number of times his foot went up and down or shuffled to the left and then right. Up down, left, right, right left, down, up.

'It may help if you…' His friend stopped talking at the site of his eyes. He looked up, his eyes narrow and piercing. He glared his friend down, now realising that his friend knew nothing.

Don't tell him a thing.

The voices in his head were really piping in, letting him know they had an opinion on it all, but of course, they always had an opinion.

It won't help, it'll only cause you more hurt.

He felt frozen on the spot. He was unsure of how to react, the voices spoke to menacingly in his ear, their words pained him.

He has no idea what you have been through, no idea what you go through every day. He doesn't deserve to know.

He swallowed hard; the tears had shifted from behind his eyes to a lump in his throat.
'There's nothing left to say,' he released finally, his voice quiet and timid but he allowed the words to slip out without another thought.
His friend sighed again, he didn't seem impatient or frustrated, he looked distressed, visibly hurt and upset. His hand met with his hair again, rustling it back and pushing it out of his eyes. He watched in awe, enticed by his friend's curly hair.
'I'm not leaving until you talk to me.' His friend's voice curt, it was firm, unmoving. He was surprised, his neck recoiled.

'You *must* leave,' he pressed.

'If you force me out, I'll tell everyone where you are.' His friend was antagonising him now. He felt rage climbing up his throat.

We told you he was trouble.

The voices were rallying. They added to his anger, they fuelled the fire that was now flickering and licking at every aspect of him.

'I will lead *everyone* here,' his friend pushed further.

'What do you want me to say?' He was screaming now, and as if a switch had been flicked, he unleashed it all. 'What will make you happy?'

He burst open at the seams he was trying so hard to hold together.

'I want you to be honest with me,' his friend said softly, 'to be honest with yourself.'

'I can't.' He groaned, throwing his head back. 'It. Hurts. Too. Much.' His voice a struggle to get out.

His friend leaned forward, closing in on his space, and touched his hand.

He recoiled instantly, standing up to get away from him.

'Don't touch me!' He screamed. 'You pretend to care; you pretend to know. Nobody does! Nobody!' He was yelling loud enough to be heard in the next valley over. His finger pointed at his friend.

'I do care,' his friend spoke with a continued softness, like honey. His friend was so very patient with him, so measured and kind. Anticipating his outbursts, prepared for the inevitable fall out.

And so, he allowed it. For once, he shut the voices up for good and he allowed his true thoughts to escape his lips. And this time, there was someone listening to them.

'Do you want me to tell you that I am not the same person I was before it happened?' The words came out as a scream. 'Do you want me to tell you that I cannot get through a day or a night without him crossing my mind, and without it bringing me every sadness? I will never be who I was before he died, I will never laugh the same, I will never smile in the same way, I will never get the same joy I once had because he was the only person who could give me those kinds of emotions.' He was crying now. 'I have never felt so comfortable with a person, and I will never be able to rebuild that feeling, or regenerate that time, I cannot recreate my childhood with someone else, he was my childhood.' He was sobbing. 'He was my upbringing; he was my best friend, he stood by me with everything that I did.' He could barely speak through the tears. 'All my mistakes he was there, every achievement I made he was the only person who truly congratulated me. He was my everything.' His body shook. His voice numbed by the tears. 'Nobody gets it, nobody understands how I can still feel like this. I will never get another childhood, another brother, I only had him and now I am alone. And people go around saying grief gets smaller and you learn to live with it but mine only increases, it gets bigger every day and it consumes me. It hurts me, it prevents me from breathing, I can't let go of it. I can't live with it.' He was shaking his head with each sob, his eyes hot and wet, his chest releasing like a balloon with a small hole in it. 'I can't ever forget him, and yet I'm terrified every day that one day I will wake up and have forgotten what he looked like or forgotten how he sounds.' He covered his eyes. 'I want to feel better; I want to feel happy again, I want to move on respectfully, without insulting him, without disregarding his memory. I am ready to move on, I am ready to continue with my life I've been patient, I've been steady, I've been the person I thought I needed to be, but I can't, I'm stuck and I'm torn and I feel guilty if I do. And now I am confused all of the time, I am lonely all of the time, I am lost. And it won't be quiet. It won't shut up. I can't seem to get rid of them. I can't shake them, they're too loud, they consume me, they have me, they own me.

'I like to remember him because I don't want to forget, but I hate remembering him all at the same time because it's too painful. I can't handle the pain anymore, this unspeakable, invisible pain, I can't, I can't, I can't. It's too painful. It hurts too much.'

18. The Man Alone with the Lake

It took them a while to clean up the mess. There was something quite peaceful about his lull, a certain comfort in rejecting his usual reticence. As soon as he had finished speaking it was as if something was unlocked, the right key was finally found and he was open, he was unveiled, he was freed from the shackles he had designed to keep himself conserved. It was as if neither boy now knew how to react, again.

But it was comforting, in his outpour he had stood and sat several times, moving with the wrecking of his body and the shaking of his tears. He was now lying on the bed, his hands over his face, but he was calm. His breathing steady as he let the anger dissipate, he let the elephant sat on his chest stand and walk away, he let deep breaths in and out.

His friend remained motionless where he sat, on the bed, just inches away from him. His friend solemn yet sad, waiting for the appropriate time to talk.

Outside there was a familiar hum from wildlife, a distant hooting of owls, a faint purr from insects and a whistling wind surrounding the cabin. It felt comfortable to be inside with his friend, for once, it was night and he was not afraid. He did not feel restricted or constrained, he felt a certain glow sitting or lying with his friend, a comfort he hadn't felt in years.

Being together with his friend gave him assurance, he liked how it felt having his friend in his cabin. He sat up and looked at his friend for the first time since he had been sobbing, he could see his friend clearly, his eyes were down at his palms, as if he was reading them for some solution.

'Come on,' his friend spoke all at once. His friend clambered up onto his feet, pulling him up at the same time. The feeling of his friends' fingers wrapped around his wrist as he pulled him to a stand.

'Where?' He resisted, his eyes sore from crying, his stomach still a pit.

'Come on,' his friend said again, continuing to hold onto his hand. Pulling him along through the door of the cabin. Out into the world.

It was darker now, still light but the sun was fading behind the trees. A milky hew from the light of the moon started to take over, slinking across the leaves and onto the craggy floor.

'No.' He froze in the door frame. His body hardening at the pull of his friend. He scowled.

His friend let out an exacerbated sigh, he was already impatient with him. 'Tom,' his friend spoke softly, like the sound of the sea curling off the sand. 'Trust me.' His friend continued. Not a question, a statement. Not a request for they both already knew it to be true.

He stopped resisting and let his friend pull him away.

Guiding him down the same path he took at least once, twice every day. Down to the lake.

His lake.

'Why are we here?' He asked, his voice brusquer than he anticipated.

His friend dropped his hand, leaving his wrist so cold from where the fingers had been.

'I cannot take the pain away, Tommy.' His friend met his eye as hard as he tried to avoid it. 'Nothing can. There is no shame in feeling how you feel.

'But you have to let it out. Keeping that sort of pain in for so many years, burns you inside.'

'I am sorry for my outburs—'

'No, I don't care about that, Tommy. Of course, I do not care. I wish you showed how you really felt more often.' His friend was ferociously shaking his head, his friend's hair falling around his face, into his eyes.

'Well, what are you saying then?' He asked.

It felt like an age before his friend spoke again. The sound of water moving to one side of them, the thin whistle of wind from their other side.

'Let it out here.' His friend said quietly, his voice barely loud enough over the sound of the environment.

'What?' He demanded, now his voice was testy.

'In here, where nobody can hear. Let it out, Tommy.' His friend repeated, gesturing to the body of water next to them. 'Trust me.' He repeated.

'In-in the water?' He asked, now sounding nervous. His friend nodded once, the sun causing his dark skin to glow. To him, his friend almost did not seem real. Like it was an illusion, another hallucination. But his friend was here, he was real.

Without thinking for another moment, he did as his friend had asked. Taking each step ever so slowly. His ankles submerged. It was ice cold, and he took in a sharp breath. For a second it reminded him of ice baths after training. His hands curled into fists, so tight his skin went bright white. He took another step forward, willing himself to continue. Until eventually he was in up to his shoulders, his whole body submerged within the cool black water.

'Let it out.' His friend shouted from the bank of the lake. He could hardly make his friend out. He was too far in, the sky now too dark. The air between them too much.

But he knew what his friend meant. His exhale was hard and long. But it made way for what he did next.

He screamed.

He screamed and screamed until he felt his throat climbing out from his mouth. His lungs burning and crying out to stop. His stomach hurting from the howling cries.

Eventually he fell forward. Face first into the water. Its cool embrace was comforting. He screamed again in the water, allowing it to flood into his mouth and nose. Filling him up entirely until that too blistered with pleasure.

It freed him.

The sound of his own cries echoing around the ravine. The sound of nothing but him and the water.

He did not know how long he was in there for. The sun completely vanished. The moon taking its place and beaming down across the water. Silvery lines rippling across the surface.

When he eventually made it out his friend was waiting for him. Sat on the bank as he often did. Just watching.

His friend wore little on his face, placid and plain.

He took a seat next to him, his body drenched, his clothes dripping with every step he took. But he felt different, he felt lighter. The same pain still wrecked his body, his mind. But it was relieved slightly, some of it relinquished into the water. It took the burden off for him.

'I'm sorry,' he said, feeling a wave of shame, it surged from his feet and made him nauseous.

As soon as the words left his tongue his friend looked up, his face shocked.

'No, Tommy, never apologise for how you feel.' His friend's face was stern. 'I'm sorry I cannot make you feel better.' He smiled weakly. His friend reverted his eyes back to his hands.

'That did make me feel better.' He admitted, his friend returned the smile. Weak as well, but it was there.

He lay back down on the bank, sighing heavily. The wind gently tapped branches from neighbouring trees against one another. He watched a small butterfly skittle about the reeds at the edge of the water before landing on the grass ahead from him, it was that same monarch butterfly he had seen six months before, perfect in every way. It had returned to him. He found himself staring at it, smiling. Then, because the door had already been opened, he found himself sharing again.

'You know,' he said, chuckling slightly at the thoughts he had. 'Sometimes I think he is still here,' he said calmly, a thought he had made peace with long ago. 'I don't really know what I believe in anymore, but I believe he is still here, keeping an eye on things.' His friend was watching him closely, catching his eyes every few words, holding them there firmly. 'I think his form changes, sometimes he's a bird, twirling and diving and swooping and soaring,' his hand danced with the movement of a bird. 'Sometimes he is the wind, a whispering, delicate wind that kind of brushes your cheek, and sometimes.' He gestured to the grass, the butterfly had flown off, not wanting to be seen by anyone other than him. He sighed, 'Sometimes he can be a butterfly, the perfect reincarnation.' His friend copied him now, lying next to him on the bank of the lake. Both boys staring up at the night sky, the scattering of stars, the glow of the white moon.

'Death is not the opposite of life but a part of it,' his friend exclaimed, turning to face him on the ground. 'His physical form may have gone, but I believe he is here too.'

He copied his movement, and they were now lying, their bodies almost touching, facing each other on the grassy bank. 'I believe in reincarnation, or not even reincarnation, but I believe souls and spirits live on. Your brother is with you, and he wouldn't want you to be like this,' he sighed, he knew all this, he knew this isn't what his brother would have wanted but this was who he was this was how he grieved his losses.

'You still have your brother you still have the childhood and the memories,' his friend continued. 'Those will never be taken from you.'

His friend was smiling, his pearly white teeth showing off in front of him.

'I want to help you; help you see that remembering memories doesn't have to be a bad thing, death can never take those memories away from you. Death can't touch the wonderful, good things about him, but you have to learn that. You have to learn that those good things are to be held onto but not so tightly you can't grab onto new things.' His friend's voice was measured, kind and peaceful, like listening to the trickling of a waterfall, the movement of a river, the sound of waves lapping the shore. He closed his eyes.

'I don't even know how to start to do that,' he admitted timidly. His eyes still clamped shut.

His friend reached out and touched his arm, resting his hand against it. He tensed up at the warmth of his friend against his body.

'Yes, the road ahead looks rough and distressed and difficult, and I can't promise that it won't be. But I will help you, I want to help you, I want you to help me. You have to let me in, Tommy.' His friend moved his hand up his arm, resting on his shoulder. 'Let me help you.'

He felt the warmth of his friends hand through his clothes. A feeling that could have been for comfort and assurance but felt intimate. It felt like more than just a friendly touch. His friend had made the decision to touch his arm.

'Me help you?' His whole body was shaking. He was not cold, though he should have been. It was from the touch, from the closeness, from the intensity.

He leaned forward and kissed his friend, it was soft at first, tentative and gentle, and then he realised he could feel no resistance so tried a little harder. He wrapped his arms around him and eventually felt a kiss back, his body was surrounded with arms, and they were pulling him closer and closer. He kissed harder and felt himself tingling everywhere inside, his body was limp, but his lips and tongue were alive and enigmatic.

Then he pulled away, it was all too much that he shuffled back and stood up. His cheeks suffused with colour.

His best friend stared back at him, unmoved, unshaken, but solemn faced. He realised he was panting and smiled coyly. He chucked breathlessly, shaking his head slightly; his friend stayed emotionless.

He got up from the bank and started to pace, his hands entwined in his hair, firstly pulling it out of the messy bun he had drawn it into and then frantically pulling his fingers through it. He would smile occasionally, and sometimes a cautious laugh would escape his lips but he continued to pace, not knowing what to say, or how to act, or what to think.

For once, he was alone in his head, his thoughts were his own. Nobody else was trying to talk to him, but he realised how much of a mess his mind was without the voices organising it for him.

'Tommy?' his friend said after what must have been at least five minutes of him pacing.

His friend had not moved but remained in the exact same position; his friend's hands were now folded neatly in his lap. He could tell that his friend had done nothing but watch him pace, but he liked that he was being watched. He liked having his friend's eyes on him.

Eventually, he stopped moving and stood at the end of his friends feet, staring his friend down. He could not help the smile creeping across his face, he could not stop it and he did not want to hide it.

'Thank you, for saying everything right,' he eventually blurted. 'You say all the right things.' He smiled. 'And you're right, I need you.' His chest felt like it was about to explode. His feet ready to take off from the ground. He was light and heavy all at the same time, confused and ecstatic all at once.

His friend sighed, and his eyes dropped back down to his hands once again.

'I had been confused about how this was home to me, this was everything for me, but something was still missing. I still felt lonely.' He was still smiling; he hadn't smiled this hard in a while.

He felt everything falling into place, he saw his future and it was wonderful. There were no pressures, no more football, no more fame and no more money, he saw his happiness creep back in, he saw his friend help him grieve, help him move on. He would live in this cabin with his friend, they would be peaceful and isolated and be able to share and talk and be free and be so, so happy.

'And now I've realised what was missing.' He felt his eyes almost brimming with tears, his body filled with excitement. 'I realise what did not feel like home.' His friend remained motionless. 'It was you; it was a piece of my last life I did not appreciate enough; I did not realise how much I needed in my life until it was gone. It was you, and I know I want you here and I need you to be in this new life with me. I need you to help me, like you said. I need to walk that treacherous path with you, by my side, and I'll help you too.' He was so unleashed he couldn't control his words in any way, he let them all come out without any regret. And then it hit him, since he had opened that door, he had not heard one single sound from the voices. They too had flooded out with his emotions, and he was left with his own thoughts, his own refreshing ideas and his head felt lighter, it felt freer. He laughed.

'I know I need you and it is because I love you' He poured out his soul, letting it rest on his sleeve, his heart exposed on his chest.

He felt bare chested, open, and vulnerable but for some reason with his friend there he felt safe, he felt protected, and he felt home.

'Tommy,' his friend said slowly, dropping his head.

He struggled to meet his friend's eye; they darted around avoiding making contact with his own.

'I know you like it here a-and you may not necessarily want to stay here. And if that is the case maybe if we see each other every so often, you can come out here to the cabin or we can take a walk in the moors together, or a swim in the lake.' He was already excited by the prospect, his new life but with the missing piece. He shook his head. 'I can't not see you for another six months.'

'Tom.' His friend reconnected their eyes again, they were more serious.

He stopped pacing about and faced his friend, his chest rising and falling quickly.

'I want to help you, and I will, everything I said before is true and honest and I believe I can help you,' his friend repeated, he nodded like an excited puppy, restless and impatient.

'But you should know…,' his friend sighed, 'I asked Beth to marry me.'

And all at once, a car had crashed into his side. A knife had ripped through his bare chest, it was tearing into his skin, exposing his heart, and slashing into it. The blade left no part of his heart alone, it was wrecked, it was unusable.

'Okay,' he said emotionlessly, feeling his heart fading into the distance.

He stepped back, stepping away from the bank, away from his friend.

'And, she said yes,' his friend continued.

He slumped down onto the floor. His head dropping to his feet for a second before he looked up at his friend and smiled.

'Congratulations,' he said, nodding to convince himself whilst he spoke.

He lifted his heart off the floor and gently tried to resuscitate it, breathing heavily, not noticing the amount he was shuddering.

'Tommy...,' his friend said, his voice pleading. His heart was in pieces, but he did a good job taping it up, he patched it together and re-slotted it back into the giant slash across his chest. 'Say something.' The reluctance was back embedded in the tone of his friend's voice.

Restoring his heart to its rightful place and protecting it once again by locking the door and completely closing himself off, his head felt heavy his chest felt tight, he barred himself in and reattached the shackles. One minute, a few words that's all it took for him to open up and then completely shut down again.

'I think it is time you were going home,' he finally said firmly, after taking his time at replacing his heart.

'No, Tommy.' His friend shook his head, exacerbated, reaching out and touching trying to touch his hand.

He moved away sharply, ignoring the now horrible tingling his friend's touch left on his skin. His throat was dry and numb, blocked by a large lump which was unmoved.

'Yes, it is time for you to leave.' He gritted his teeth.

His friend watched him carefully, he shook away the feeling of tears in his eyes and burrowed a harrowing look at his friend.

'And I told you everything you wished to hear, so you cannot tell anyone about this place,' his friend continued to shake his head, he was trembling but stood firm. 'You cannot make me come home.' He added firmly. Gesturing for his friend to stand.

'Tom,' his friend sounded desperate but he remained face stony and cold. His jaw tightly locked. 'I would never force someone to return if they did not want.' His friend said definitively. 'And I will not tell a soul.'

'Thank you,' he said grimly, 'you may take my car, I shan't be needing it anymore.'

Eventually, his friend stood. He stepped back as his friend moved closed. Retreating like he was afraid. His friend dropped his head and turned.

He dropped to the floor and waited, watching the floor. Listening out for the sound of the car engine splutter on, the brightness of the headlights illuminating in the distance, and the crunching of the leaves and branches as the car turned around and drove away.

Finally, he was alone again. His head resting against the soft ground beneath him. it steadied him, his breathing ragged. Just him, alone with the lake.

He let his emotions escape again, but he was so lost and so hurt that his sobs barely mustered a sound. A single tear rolled down his cheek and hung off his chin, resting there until he wiped it away.

But why should he be upset? He never told his friend about how he felt, never spoke to him, the only thing he had actually done was kiss him once six months ago and then he left and did not speak to him again.

So why should his friend wait for him?

It was hardly even unexpected, his friend had been seeing the same girl, Beth, ever since they had been sixteen, it was expected. He would have been confused; no, he would have assumed nothing less than for them to get married. And yet, he was still upset. He still had the intense burning in his stomach, like his organs were being set alight from the inside out, an animal chewing their way through the cooked meat inside, crashing through each organ not caring about the hurt and damage it was doing. He had allowed his friend to see his scars, his torment, his pain. He had allowed himself to become comfortable and let his friend convince him he could be salvaged; he could be saved.

Was he ever his friend?

He had lost two things in his life, his brother and now his friend.

He had lost love in both; he had lost hope in both. His love, his one true love, and the love of his brother, and now he understood that this, this feeling he was experiencing, was what people meant when they said they felt alone.

And within a second he leapt up, running towards his home. His cabin. He flew the door open and ran for his bed. Throwing himself on it, his legs splayed across the sheets, and pulled out his notebook.

Today – today confirmed my feelings and decisions were all correct. Today I am certain that I have done the right thing.

And with that Tommy closed the book, letting the pencil be squashed within the thick, disorganised, stained pages and he stepped off from the bed. Reshuffling the duvet so it was pristine he left the cabin and planned to do that every day for the rest of his life.